Goat Girl

Sylvia Morrow

Chapter Notes

This is a story about a man and a woman who become romantically involved with one another despite some pretty significant differences between them. The world around them is both the same and different from ours in ways that will become obvious as you read, but one thing that doesn't change is that people can be bigots. People treat our main character terribly because of who she is throughout the book, so this is a warning for those who may be triggered by that. The story also briefly touches on discussions of abuse and cheating (outside of the relationship our two main characters are in with each other), poverty, and depression.

For any additional content information, please check the Sylvia Morrow content page at
https://sylviamorrowbooks.carrd.co/

Chapter One

Jill

"Hey, Jill. Focus. Sandra will be super ticked off if she catches you eating her daisies again."

Snapping to attention after having drifted off into a daydream, I find my mouth full of flowers. *Aww dang, not again.* Every day, my boss leaves bouquets of fresh flowers on the counter here at the café, and at least once a week, I end up chomping away on them.

It's only to be expected; I'm half goat, after all.

I swallow the petals and quickly try to rearrange the remaining flowers, so the vase doesn't look quite so empty, then step back from the counter to assess my work.

"How's that look?"

Mary bites the inside of her cheek as she looks it over. After a few seconds, she leans in to adjust a few violets and take out some of the ruined stems.

"There. Looks fine now. Just please use the other register so you're not in chewing distance next time, okay?"

She laughs as I cover my face. I *am* embarrassed, but it could be worse; aggressive headbutting or something else equally distressing could be one of my traits instead. Distracted eating of flora is a much better option.

"Deal. Here come some folks now, anyway. Slide over and give me register two."

A group of smiling people walks through the door. It's a lovely fall day, perfect for pumpkin spice lattes and cinnamon tea. People are often in a good mood when they come in these first days of autumn to get their favorite seasonal drinks.

Their smiles falter when they see me, the mood shifting dramatically. Usually, customers don't react this way. Most people are accepting of those like me, thankfully, but not everyone is. Not these people.

The two couples swerve from the direction they were headed, going from my register to Mary's register. The women attempt to keep smiles on their faces, obviously fake, but the men don't even bother. They order their drinks and pay in cash. When the man paying glances at the tip jar, he turns to Mary and hands her the money directly instead of putting the change inside it.

"This is for *you*, honey. Get you something good. People like *us* got to take care of each other."

With that, they walk to the far end of the counter, over to where our quiet coworker, Bill, makes their drinks.

Mary stands there with the money in her hand, biting the inside of her cheek, eyes wide and watery. I grind my jaw, furry ears flicking in agitation. She tosses the cash into the jar.

"Screw those people, Jill. You know we love you. I'm sorry I didn't say anything. I got caught off guard."

"I know. I understand."

And I do. She's not built to recognize the signs like I am. When he said that to her, it probably really did shock her. But not me. I wrap my arms around my chest and give myself a little hug.

"It's cool. I'm going to go in the back and do dishes while it's slow, if that's alright. I'm not feeling like being out here right now."

"Oh, that's totally fine, Jill! Take your time!"

The customers from earlier exit the café, watching me and murmuring amongst themselves as they go.

"Thanks, Mary. Tell me if you need me to do anything else while I'm back there."

When I get into the back, I toss on a rubber apron and fill up the dish sink. The tears that used to come when something like that happened don't fall this time. I just wash the dishes and daydream about a better life, one with smiles that don't falter and flowers that don't get me into trouble.

Chapter Two

Jill

I SET MY BAG on the table next to the front door of the little apartment I share with my mom, slip off my work shoes, and toss my jacket onto the loveseat. My mom will certainly gripe at me about that, but I'm too tired to put it in the closet, despite it being only a few feet away. Instead, I plop down on the tattered sofa, which is not too far from the door, and switch on the television.

"Still no word about Captain Whiz's whereabouts, Jim?" asks the bubbly blonde news anchor.

Bleh, more Superhero talk on the news. Ever since The Big Mash-Up, it seems like that's all anyone talks about. God, I hate that name—*The Big Mash-Up*. Couldn't they have thought of something better for an event that changed the entire world as we know it?

"Not yet, Claire. I'm sure we'll know more soon. Next up, we have news on another beloved Hero. Honor Man is visiting the Capitol tomorrow. We'll have details on that and more after the break."

I switch off the TV with a groan. *Freaking Honor Man*. I'm thankful that he stopped Darkiss, the one responsible for me being half goat—but do I have to hear about him every day, even four years later? A person can only take so much.

"Jill?" my mom calls from the kitchen. "Is that you?"

"Nope, I'm a Villain who broke into the house to watch the news."

"Don't be rude." She pads into the room in her old, pink house slippers and pauses, hands on her hips. "How was your day?"

"Fine. Mostly. There was one group of jerks, but they weren't too bad. I accidentally ate the daisies again, though." A grimace screws up my face.

"Well, you just need to get your darn head out of the clouds, and you'll be fine." She waves her yellow, dish-gloved hand in my direction.

Then, she shakes her head and, in a slightly deeper voice, says, "Leave her alone, Cristina. Kids need to daydream."

She stomps her foot and says, in her normal voice, "She's twenty-seven years old, that's hardly a kid. Now, get out of our business."

My mom was one of the more than ninety-five percent of people who got mashed with another human during The Big Mash-Up. People who got mashed up didn't combine bodies; one person kept their body, and the other was absorbed into them, only to exist as a second consciousness—another mind without the brain. My mom's lucky because she got the body, but unlucky since there are *still* two people in her head: her and my uncle Sal. Most people were able to be separated once Honor Man defeated Darkiss, and they got the cure worked out, but a very small portion of people stayed stuck. She and Uncle Sal just happened to be in that group.

I, on the other hand, am one of the less than five percent that got mashed with an animal—or "Mashies" as people call us. *None* of us were able to be separated, and *all* of us inherited animal features. Thankfully, I retained all of my mind and gained very little of the goat's personality. I did get some physical features, but not enough to be disabling. Some people weren't so lucky.

"What was that on the news about Honor Man? He's coming here? Did I hear right?" My mom asks.

"Yeah, I guess. Who cares?"

I slump in my seat and cross my arms. My mom is a big Honor Man fan. Most people are.

"Yeah, who cares? We hear about him all the time. Bah," says Uncle Sal from my mom's mouth.

"Who cares? *Who cares?* That's the man who saved us from destruction! Who knows what could have happened if he hadn't stopped you-know-who!" my mom's voice comes back. "Imagine if Darkiss had gone beyond Capital City. The whole world could have been destroyed!"

Her hands are back on her hips now, her brow lowered disapprovingly.

"Okay, Mom. Whatever. I'm going to shower and head to bed. I already ate at work. I'm working the opening shift tomorrow, so I need the rest."

"You worked a closing shift, then you open to-morrow? That's no fun!"

I stand and stretch my aching back.

"Nope, but bills gotta get paid. Love you, Mom."

My mom and Uncle Sal haven't been able to find a job in a while, so I'm currently the sole provider here. With them still together, and me a Mashie, this household isn't getting tons of high-paying job offers right now.

I give her a kiss on the cheek and head to my room to grab some clean pajamas, then to the shower. The hot water feels fantastic on my sore muscles. Standing all day is taking a toll on my body, and I can't imagine doing this for the rest of my life. Running the farm never made me feel like this, even when I worked my hardest.

I scrub my stubby little tail and my short horns and take just one second to feel sorry for myself. Just one. Then I breathe deeply and move on, like I keep having to do.

Chapter Three

Liam

"Hey, I gotta bring Lisa that dumb-ass pumpkin drink thing. Hold up a sec," Frank says as he turns into the parking lot of Sandra's Café.

I haven't been to this place in years because I'm not a big coffee drinker. To be real, I mostly drink too many energy drinks and then just a bunch of water to make sure I don't get dehydrated. It's bad for me, but a man's got to stay awake somehow when he works long shifts. And I admit I just really like the taste of the pink-flavored one. Frank gives me shit about that, but he's an asshole.

We open the door and see that there are two lines in front of us, one longer than the other by a pretty wide margin. We get into the shorter line because obviously we do. Who wants to wait longer? That would be dumb. Frank is ahead of me, so while I'm waiting, I poke around at all the trinkets for sale—mugs and cards and coffee beans. *Beans*, ha. I'm a simple man, and that word always makes me smile. I don't know why, and I don't care, but it's funny.

It doesn't take long for the line to clear. I look up at the cashier, still not entirely sure what to order.

She's the most beautiful person I've ever seen.

I find myself unable to form a thought beyond "girl pretty, want to kiss." She's saying something, but it doesn't register; no sound comes through. I'm totally lost in her super strange eyes. They're *yellow,* and the pupils are...square? I've seen this before on something. Where?

Oh yeah, a *goat.* I notice her ears then, too, black furry ears that blend into her hair. And horns. *Actual Horns.*

She's a Mashie. I don't know any Mashies. I'd really like to get to know *her,* though. In a very intimate way.

SLAM!

Something whacks the counter in front of me. *Her hand.*

"Hey! If you're not going to order, I need you to please move. There is a line behind you, sir."

The spell is finally broken, and I see that the girl in front of me is now clearly pissed off, her face deep red in anger. I don't know how long I've been standing here staring at her, but it must have been uncomfortably long.

Aww shit, she probably thinks I was staring at her because she's a Mashie, not because she's hot. *Liam, you're a moron.*

"Fruit drink, please," I say like an imbecile before clearing my throat and attempting to make actual sense. "What do you have that's, uh, fruity?"

She blinks those big, yellow eyes at me a few times before answering, the redness in her tan cheeks fading.

"Do you want something hot or cold?"

"Cold. I'm not a hot drinks kind of guy. Just a man that doesn't drink coffee, here at the coffee shop."

Okay. Getting back on track. Talking normally now, even if it's awkward as shit.

"I've got a great strawberry smoothie. We can even add a shot of our new energizing formula to wake you up this morning if you'd like. No more staring blankly at the cash register."

She smiles now, the angry red gone completely.

"Sorry about the staring. I'm slow at, uh, talking." I cringe at myself, nervously ruffling my hair. *Yep, about as smooth as a gravel road, buddy.* I shake my head and keep trying. "The smoothie sounds perfect, actually. You're good at this. Next time I don't know what I wanna drink, I'm coming here to ask you."

She *giggles,* and a dimple appears on her left cheek. A dimple. *Oh my god, I'm in love.*

"I look forward to it."

She swipes my card, then gives it and the receipt back to me.

"See you soon, I hope. Bill will have your drink at the other end."

She gives me a little wave, which I return before reluctantly walking away. *She hopes to see me soon.* Is that just polite employee speak, or does she like me? I'll have to come in again and find out, I guess.

Wait, is that creepy, trying to talk to a girl at her job? People say you aren't supposed to hit on women while they're working. But what if you're destined to be together? What if she says she wants you to come back? Why is this shit so hard? *Damn it.* Whatever, I'm coming back, and I'll just try not to be weird about it.

I grab my drink when it's finished, and Frank and I head out. I want to say goodbye, or at least wave again to that girl, but she's too busy to notice me, so we just go.

When we get outside, Frank turns to me and grins in a way that I know means he's about to give me shit.

"So, what happened back there? Looked like you were talking to the barista. She's a Mashie, though, huh? Wild."

For some reason, I don't like that he's bringing up that she's a Mashie. I don't even know why it bothers me. It just makes my skin itch.

"Yeah, I don't know. She's cute. I have zero skill at picking up women, though. It's whatever," I reply as we get into the car.

I take a sip of my smoothie and then set it in the drink holder, hoping Frank lets the topic drop. Of course, he doesn't.

"You want to go back and see if you can get her number? Get you some action for once? Get some tail? Get it? Tail?"

"No, she's working, and you're gross. Just drive, you have a girlfriend to bring a drink to, and I have to get to work. The bugs don't research themselves."

Frank stares me down with the shit-eating grin for a few more seconds before starting the car and backing out of the parking lot.

He drops me off at the facility where I work, currently for a project studying arthropods to help Sir Cicada in his efforts to heal the city. I accomplish very little all day, however. My mind is far too occupied by thoughts of furry ears and yellow eyes.

Chapter Four

Jill

"Hey, Jill, take the register. That guy you said was cute yesterday is coming in."

I stop wiping down the espresso machine and scurry over to switch spots with Sarah, my morning coworker. Smoothing my apron, I watch the door as the guy from yesterday walks through, his lips rosy from the cold air and his caramel-brown hair fluttering in the breeze like a freaking model. *Liam;* I remember his name from his credit card. Yeah, it's a little Psycho Sally to eyeball a cute guy's card for his name, but, eh, I couldn't help it. Not when he's this *fine*.

"Hello again! Can't decide what to drink today?" I ask as he approaches the register.

It's a pretty slow time in the late morning, and he's the only one in line. Plenty of time for chit-chat.

"Yeah, you got it. Energy drinks aren't cutting it after that fantastic smoothie yesterday. What else you got for me? Something different."

He rubs his stubble-free chin in an exaggerated thinking expression. I notice his hands are large and well taken care of. Not manicured per se, but clean, and his nails trimmed. He's not dressed in a suit or in anything fancy, but he looks nice: black fitted pants, a gray wool jacket, and a red, plaid scarf. The outfit is classic fall perfection.

"Do you like tea at all?"

"Yeah, sweetened. Iced. And fruity, of course."

With a laugh, I nod.

"Of course, of course. An iced peach black tea is what you need. I know you'll like it."

"Give me a large one then." He pauses to read my name tag. "Jill."

He hands me his credit card, and I glance at it as if to read his name. As if it wasn't already running through my mind all night.

"You got it, Liam."

After the transaction is complete, he goes to the other end of the counter to wait for his drink. I can't help but peek at him occasionally, and every time I do, he's looking back at me, though I can tell he's trying to hide it.

My stubby tail wags about a million miles an hour, no matter how hard I try to get it to stop. When I catch him noticing it, he breaks out in a huge grin. The damn thing wags when I get too excited—or just whenever it wants—and I have no control over it. With my face now on fire, I slap my hands over it to try to hide my embarrassed expression. When I uncover it, he's no longer at the other end of the counter but instead right in front of my register.

"If you're working tomorrow, I'll see you then, Jill," he says, leaning toward me.

The light coming in through the windows makes his bright blue eyes seem to almost glow, they're so vi-brant, and the golden highlights in his light brown hair shine. I have to really hold myself back from sighing.

"I won't be in until the evening shift, so you might miss me, but I'll be here."

"We'll see. I might be thirsty tomorrow evening. Have a good day."

He takes a sip of his drink as he opens the door, his face lighting up.

"That's good as hell, Jill. I'll see you soon."

Then he walks away. Can *soon* come as soon as possible?

Chapter Five

Liam

"I'm telling you, man, I think she likes me too. She was smiling and stuff. Not like a cashier's smile, but a real smile. I don't know. It was so cute."

Frank and I are gaming, as we often do in the evenings. He's shot me about a million times tonight as we talk over our headsets. Normally, I kick his ass, but I can't focus tonight thinking about Jill.

"So weird hearing you wanting to date again. Thought you were gonna be Mister Lonely forever."

"Yeah, well, she's special. I can tell."

I haven't dated in years, and I really wasn't interested in it anymore. But I'm not kidding when I say Jill is different. There's something about her that draws me in.

"She looks like she's got nice tits under that apron and everything, but she's a Mashie. I don't know, though, maybe you just like them exotic. Taking a walk on the wild side. *Wildlife* side," Frank says as he shoots me in the head yet again.

Okay. That pissed me off.

"Shut up, Frank. That's not why."

"You know, I heard male goats piss on themselves to attract female goats. Maybe you could try that before you go in next time. By the way, do you think she bleats when she comes? Like *baaahh? Mmm, yeah, baaaah!*"

He starts cracking up. My hands grip the controller so hard I'm surprised it doesn't break.

"Fuck you. That's some bullshit. Piss on your own self, asshole."

I switch off the console and fling my headset down to the floor. *Fucking prick.* I knew Frank could be a little bit of a dick sometimes, but he's generally a cool guy. Guess I never really talked to him about his thoughts on Mashies, though.

Actually, now that I think about it, I have heard him say dumb shit before. It just never really fazed me. The Mashie jokes seemed pretty harmless, but...*shit.* I'm an asshole for not saying something sooner, aren't I?

I lay back on the sofa with my hands in my lap in the quiet for a bit, thinking of all the times I could have said something and didn't. *Yeah, I'm an asshole.* All I can do is be better now, I guess.

Seeing how late it's gotten, I stand and stretch my back. I'm sore from standing all day in the lab. Today was a busy day with all the breakthroughs in the Sir Cicada research. It's a really exciting time at work, but even that is overshadowed by thoughts of Jill.

I get ready for bed quickly and lie down, happy to fall asleep. The sooner I wake up, the closer I get to seeing her.

Chapter Six

Jill

CAN'T SLEEP AT ALL. My brain will *not* shut up, which is ridiculous, considering how much I've worked recently, and how tired I am because of it. I just keep thinking about that Liam guy and how I can't wait to see him. I even caught myself daydreaming about mounting him before realizing that it was a goat instinct creeping in, *ugh*. I mean, that realization didn't stop the thoughts from playing out, but I'm not sure I'm ready to process that bit of new information about myself quite yet. For now, I'll just try to be my best self for him next time I see him.

My nails are filed and buffed perfectly, I waxed my beard stubble (*ugh*, more goat stuff), trimmed my split ends off, and made sure my nicest uniform clothes are clean. I'm going to look good tomorrow, so help me. And then I am going to make a move on him.

I turn on the television since I have nothing better to do this late at night. It's either that or mess around on the internet, and lord knows I do enough of that already. Maybe there will be a funny movie on or something.

"Now, with Villain-Be-Gone, you can protect any house from any Villain with one simple trick!"

Ugh, infomercials. Not sure how they're even allowed to sell that stuff. Villains are *people*, not pests you can just keep away with a trap or spray. Besides, after Honor Man caught Darkiss, The Bureau for the Management and Study of Aberrant Genetics locked the other Villains up inside Gnistra Lakes Penitentiary. They'll never get out of there. I change the channel because, *no thanks,* and try again.

"And it looks like the weather is going to be wonderful today, Jim, thanks to the return of Captain Whiz."

Argh, more news. I switch off the TV and go back to my bedroom, get into bed, and turn on my laptop. Guess it's back to poking around online. My cheap, thin pillows do a crappy job of propping me up, so I end up just sitting against the headboard and holding the laptop on my knees.

An idea pops into my head. When I looked at Liam's credit card, I saw his last name. *What if I looked him up?* Okay, I know it's unethical to do that, but it's not *that* bad, right? Just a little peek? I bite my lip and hover my hands over the search bar before deciding, *screw it,* and going for it.

Liam Jemison.

I search for just a bit before finally coming across a wide-open social media profile. You'd think by now he would know to make everything private, but I guess some people are just too trusting.

Alright, let's see. What can we find out about Liam?

He's twenty-five. *Ooh, I'm a cradle robber, ha.*

He's an entomologist. I quickly search up what the heck that is and find out it's someone who studies bugs, basically. I've never been too afraid of bugs, so that's alright. *Let's see what's next.*

Doesn't list any religion or political affiliation. That's ok, if he doesn't bother listing it, then it probably means he's not some kind of zealot, which is just fine with me.

Scrolling through his timeline, I find that he's shared lots of links to charity organizations, mostly for animal and children's rights. That's pretty sweet. Some memes actually make me laugh. A good sense of humor is important.

I don't see any pictures of ex-girlfriends, at least as far back as I scroll, which is several years. That could mean a lot of different things, some good and some bad. *Hmm.*

What I don't see is anything anti-Mashie or anything that is pro-Separate Species Party. The Separate Species Party is a small, but growing, political group that wants to label Mashies a different species from humans to take our voting rights away, as well as other rights like the right to own property or marry, and so on. If he belonged to that party, it would obviously be a deal breaker, so I breathe a sigh of relief.

When I'm about to close the page, I decide to look a little longer. I'm still not tired, and there really just isn't anything else I want to do.

I poke through his past profile pictures and find a recent one where he looks extra adorable. His blue eyes are bright and sparkling, and his brown hair falls over his brow. His hand reaches up to smooth that hair out of the way, showcasing those thick, well-cared-for fingers.

I think of those hands against my cheek, caressing my face, and I imagine they're soft. It's been so, so long since anyone has touched me like that, and if he did, I think I would just die on the spot. If he stroked down my face to my neck, across my shoulder, lowering the straps on my dress...

Oh god. My heart is racing just thinking about it. I shut the laptop and set it on my bedside table, then hide under my comforter. Right now, he's just a customer, and that's super freaking inappropriate to think thoughts like that.

But if he becomes more than a customer...

Shivering, I bury myself further into the blankets. I need to get to sleep as fast as possible. Tomorrow can't come soon enough.

Chapter Seven

Liam

ALRIGHT, SO MAYBE IT'S extra creepy, but I'm waiting in the parking lot for there to be no customers in line before I go into the café. I feel like a stalker sitting here sunk in my seat just watching her through the front window, but there's no way I'm going in there with other people surrounding me. Not when I'm going to ask her out.

Because I *am* going to ask her out. I'm determined to.

I don't even care if it's creepy anymore, to be honest. I think if I weren't sure there was a mutual vibe between us, then I wouldn't do it, but there definitely is. The more I think about it, the more I'm sure of it. *Ugh, I hope I'm not wrong.*

After about ten minutes of sitting here like I'm in a god damn stakeout, the line ends, and business seems to quiet down for the time being. *Now's my chance.*

I step out of the car and blow out a deep breath that turns white in the crisp evening air. My stomach is threatening to toss my lunch back at me, but I take another deep breath, and things settle down. No more time to wait, here we go.

When I open the door, I'm hit with warmth and the combined scent of cinnamon, milk, chocolate, and coffee that's now become my favorite fragrance. Jill's back is turned to me, and I wish I could see her adorable tail, but it's blocked by the cash register. I walk toward said register until I make it to the counter. Jill turns, a customer-friendly smile on her face that transforms into a much warmer one when she recognizes me.

"Liam! You came!"

She bounces excitedly, and I can't help but let a quick laugh escape before replying. Yeah, I came. *I came hard about three times last night thinking of her.*

"That I did! I think I'm addicted to this place. It's a serious problem."

"Oh yes, very serious," she says with faux concern. "It's the coffee beans that are addicting. Beans are a magical fruit, you know. There's a whole song."

She made a beans joke. She's the perfect woman.

Jill sets her elbows on the counter and lays her head on top of them, black ponytail falling over her shoulder.

"I'm about to go on break. Would it be weird if I asked you to join me?"

My eyes go wide. Did she just ask *me* to join her? Meaning I don't need to make the first move? *Nice.*

"You're just contributing to my addiction, making me like this place even more. Terrible of you, really. But of course, I'll join you."

She grins broadly and quickly takes my drink order (peach tea) before running into the employees' room to take off her apron. When she returns, my eyes widen again at the sight of her newly revealed figure.

With the apron on, she was hot, but *damn,* when her figure is actually showing more, she's *fine as hell.*

And she's just in a polo shirt and black work pants, looking so good, so I can only imagine what's hiding underneath all that.

Actually, I'm not going to imagine that right now. I need to be able to concentrate on the conversation and not my cock. I let her lead the way to a free table and look very specifically at the back of her head and not her round, thick ass (and adorable tail) as we go.

"Hoo, I'm so glad to be off my feet for a bit," she says as she sits at the table. "I've been working crazy hours lately, and I'm starting to feel like I have the body of a ninety-year-old."

"I get that. I'm an entomologist, and I've been overseeing research that's had some breakthroughs lately and had to work overtime more than once."

I pause to check her expression. Insects bother a lot of people, and I should probably see how she feels about them right off the bat.

"Bugs don't bug you, do they?"

"Oh no, not unless they're deadly or parasites or something," she answers with a dismissive wave of her hand.

"Okay, cool. It's tough to have a job that grosses a lot of people out. Everyone else talks about things they're passionate about, but if I go to mention the award-winning study I did on the rhinoceros beetle, it's 'Eew, Liam, no one wants to hear about your horny bug.'"

Jill covers her mouth with her hands and barks out a loud laugh. She uncovers her mouth, revealing that dimple alongside her smile.

"Well, I'd let you tell me about your horny bug."

"Well, I'd let you talk to me about your passions, too. Is coffee your passion?"

With a deep frown, she takes a sip of her water.

"No, not at all. I mean, I like it and everything, but it's just a job. My dream was running my little farm. And I had it for a while, too. But then the whole mash thing happened, and everything just..." she points to her horns, "Yeah. No more farm."

"I'm sorry you lost your farm. I hope you can have one again someday."

"Thanks. I'm determined to."

"I believe in you."

We sit in silence for a moment before she speaks up.

"Would you like to go out sometime? On a date, I mean? Is that super nerdy to say date? Ugh, I'm terrible at this."

She runs her hand through her hair as her broad nose scrunches in a cringe.

"I am extremely happy you asked, to be honest, so I don't care how it sounds. I was going to ask you, anyway."

My heart is racing about ten million miles a second. This is going better than I could have planned by far.

She sits up straighter and claps her hands once, no longer cringing.

"Oh, thank goodness. Just give me your number, and we can make plans."

"I am incredibly hyped, you don't even know," I say around the world's biggest grin as I get out my phone.

We exchange numbers and make small talk about her closing shift at work before her break is over far too quickly.

"Okay, I'll text you very soon," I say on my way out the door.

"I can't wait," she replies as she waves goodbye.

Considering I'm practically itching to text her by the time I make it to my car, I have a feeling she won't have to wait long.

Chapter Eight

Jill

THE SCENT OF TAMALES drifts toward my nose as soon as I walk into my apartment. My mouth waters.

"Mom! Uncle Sal! I'm home!" I call. "I smell food, and I want it."

"Maybe if you speak to your mother a little more politely, you can have some," Uncle Sal shouts back in my mother's deepened voice.

Chuckling, I walk to the kitchen, where I find my mom standing at the counter, making me a plate. Cheese and jalapeño tamales, with beans and rice on the side, and a soda to drink.

"You made my favorite dinner tonight. I'm the luckiest girl in the world."

I kiss my mom on the cheek as I take my food.

"The world is lucky to have you- more like it," my mom says with a grin. "Now eat up. You've worked a lot lately, too much, and you need to keep up your strength."

"You know your great aunt Hana worked as a strong woman in a circus," Uncle Sal says.

He flexes mom's arms, showing chubby biceps in a short-sleeved, flowered dress.

"No, she did not," my mom says, lowering her arms.

"Yes, she did," Uncle Sal argues, flexing her arms again. "She could have easily lifted both of us in one hand, no sweat, right over her head."

"Well, now that part is close to true," my mother says, walking to the sink and putting on her yellow dish gloves. "She was very strong. But she certainly didn't work in a circus. She was a farmer, like you are."

"Like I was." I sigh around a bite of rice.

"Like you are," says Uncle Sal. "You'll be back to it, don't worry, Jilly."

"Thanks, Sal."

I take my plate into the living room and sit in front of the television where a sitcom about a Mashie-human couple is playing. The Mashie on the show is a dog, which is the second most common type after cats.

See, when Darkiss did the whole mashing people together thing, some folks who were touching a mammal at the time, if they weren't near a person, got mashed with it. Since people are often with their dogs and cats...well, there are a lot of dog and cat Mashies. I, unfortunately, was milking a goat.

Shows like this sitcom take Mashies and make them act more like animals than we actually do. Like this character wants to pee on bushes and stuff, when no one with so few dog features would actually want to do that. It's all played for laughs, but it makes us look bad.

I switch the channel to a romantic drama that's all humans and nothing related to Superheroes, or Villains, or Mashies, or anything I don't want to think about. I eat my dinner in peace and feel calm for once.

When I'm done, I take my plate to the sink and wash it by hand; dishwashers don't come with apartments in neighborhoods like this. With a full stomach and tired bones, I head to my room. I check my phone and see that Liam has texted me. If I had expected him to text so soon, I would have had my phone on me. *Argh.*

Liam: Hey, Jill! How's it going? Hope I'm not bugging you.

Aaaaaaaaaah! Okay, be cool, Jill.

Me: It's going. Just finished eating dinner. You're not bugging me at all. I think you'd know about bugs, though, wouldn't you, Mr. Entomologist? How are you?

Okay, that was corny, but safe. I stare at my phone and bite my lip. The blue light seems to blind me as I wait for ages for him to reply, though in reality, it probably only takes about thirty seconds before the telltale moving dots show me he's there.

Liam: Haha. I'm fine, great actually.

Liam: I was wondering if you wanted to go out the day after tomorrow. If you're not working, I mean.

I quickly check my schedule in my head.

Me: I work until 4 that day. What time were you thinking?

Liam: Is seven too early for dinner?

Three hours to get ready. I can do that.

Me: Sounds just right to me. Can you pick me up?

Liam: Sure! We'll do you live?

Liam: Where* oops.

Me: 1775 Lindale Ave. Do you know where that is?

Liam: I can easily find it.

Me: Should I dress up or down? What should I wear?

Liam: You'd look great in anything. But we're going to a nice place to eat if that makes a difference.

Me: You're so sweet, haha. And sounds good. Can't wait to see you!

Liam: Same here. Goodnight, Jill.

Me: Night-night!

Chapter Nine

Liam

I CHECK MY TEXTS on my break, and they're mostly the usual stuff. My mom asks how I'm doing, my cousin wants to know if my dad is going to be in town, etc. Nothing exceptional other than a message from Frank that has my jaw clenching.

Frank: Hey, man. You really mad?

I debate whether or not to text him back. I know he's on break at this time, too. I've been friends with him for most of a decade, and we know each other pretty well, so I decide that I should give him a chance to apologize. People can change.

Me: Yeah, I am.

He replies almost instantly.

Frank: Because I made a joke about goat girl? It's not that serious bro lmao

Okay, maybe they don't change that fast.

> **Me**: Maybe it's more about you being a fucking bigot. I thought you were cool and then you say shit like that.

> **Frank**: Quit being a pussy. You get one crumb of female attention since Jennifer and you're ready to give up a friendship OVER A JOKE? What the fuck?

> **Me**: Yeah I'm done here.

Blocked. There's no fucking way he had to add to the bullshit by also bringing *Jennifer* into it. Not after...well, he knows how much that hurts. I can't believe I never caught how much of a dick he was before this.

I tear into my turkey sandwich and choke down a bite before having to toss it. There's no way I can eat anymore. My stomach is in knots after that text exchange. It twists with guilt at ever having stood around while shit was said before and sadness at losing a friend. Whatever. I take a drink of my orange soda and let the sugar calm my nerves.

At least tomorrow will be better. Tomorrow I'll see Jill. My scowl relaxes when I think of her. If just thinking of her relaxes me, then texting her might help even more. That's my excuse, anyway. So, I pick up my phone. I send her a quick text just to let her know she's on my mind. She's always on my mind, it seems.

Chapter Ten

Jill

Ah, only a little left of my shift this afternoon before I can leave to go shopping for my date. I have never been more thankful that I did a close-open. When I get new clothes, I have to have them tailored around my tail, so it takes a little longer than most people's shopping does. Being on the morning shift today is perfect.

I'm wiping down a table when a little girl, maybe only three years old at the most, and her mother walk into the shop. Mary is in the back doing dishes, so it's up to me to go to the register.

"I'll be right there!" I tell them with a smile.

As I walk past them, the little girl grabs hold of my apron and looks me up and down.

"How come you are like that?" She asks in a curious tone.

There's no meanness in her squeaky voice, only pure curiosity.

"Like what?" I ask cheerfully, crouching down to her level. I love kids and don't mind answering their questions. When they're this small, they're so open and honest, but it's without cruelty.

34

She pets one of my ears, runs her little fingers along my horn, and puts her hand on the side of my face near my eyes.

"Like that."

The little girl's mother's face turns white as a ghost as she scrambles to grab her child.

"I'm so sorry, I'm so embarrassed. Sweetie, you can't just be rude to people."

The mother scoops up the girl and gives me an apologetic grimace.

"It's okay," I chuckle. "It's natural for them to be curious if they haven't met someone like me."

I go to the register, take their order, and they take a seat at a table. I go back to wiping tables across the way from them a little, trying to finish this last bit before I head out. Their conversation, however, distracts me from my work.

"Okay, let mama tell you about what happened to the lady, so you don't bother anyone else," she begins, handing the little girl some crayons and a coloring book.

My ears perk up. People talk about this stuff a lot in bits and pieces, but I've never heard the full tale as told to a child from a historical perspective. This will be interesting.

"Four years ago, that's before you were born, people didn't know there were Superheroes and Supervillains like we do now."

"Not even Lady Alpaca?" the little girl asks as she squirms in her seat.

Lady Alpaca is a cartoon character shown on public television. She's an alpaca Mashie, and, though controversial among adults, is popular among young children.

"Not even her! We didn't know at all until a really bad guy called Darkiss took over all the TV and told everyone. And he didn't just talk. He did a very bad thing."

"He was naughty?"

"He was very naughty. He decided there were too many people and that they were hurting the earth. So, he said, two people would be mashed up into one person."

"I don't get it. He smushed them?"

"No, not smushed. It's like...so, let's say you have two people. You make one person's body disappear, but their mind goes in and joins the other person's mind. So now, instead of two bodies and two minds, you have one body and two minds."

"Like when I was in your belly?" the little girl asks before taking a drink out of a sippy cup.

The mom laughs and takes a drink of her coffee before answering.

"Well, sort of. But anyway, the bad guy's powers were really strong—that's how he could do that to so many people. But they weren't perfect. There was a side effect that made it so some people got mashed up with animals. It didn't happen to many people, and no one really knows why it did, but that's what happened to the nice lady who works here.

"The people who got mashed up with other people were able to be fixed by scientists—well, most of them anyway—once Honor Man defeated Darkiss. The animal Mashies never got fixed, though."

"That's sad, right?"

"I think it depends on the person. Most would say yes, but I hear some people like how they are now. But, you know, a lot of people are mean to them."

"How come?"

"Some people are just mean to others who are different. We don't act like that, though, do we?"

"Nope! We're nice guys! Like Lady Alpaca!"

The little girl bounces in her seat, happily scribbling away in her coloring book. She then changes the topic and begins to talk about the cartoon they're watching, so I tune out.

It was good for me to hear that, I think. I really hope that's how history is being told to kids, and that the younger generation is all as accepting as that little girl.

As I work, I can't help thinking about the girl's last question—about why people are mean to us. Her mom gave her an age-appropriate answer, of course, but the truth is much more complicated. There are the same old sorry excuses for bigotry that people always trot out: fear of the unknown, religion, political control, stuff like that. But every time a large group chooses a new, smaller group to focus their hatred on, they put their own special spin on it. A little fresh pizazz added to the old bigotry to dazzle the population.

I think certain politicians want us to lose our property, businesses, etc., so that they, and their wealthy constituents, can scoop them up. They spread propaganda through memes, commercials, basically anything that shows animals doing disgusting things. Then they say that we're just like that. Disgust does more to change people's political views than one would think.

Mostly, though, when it really comes down to it, there's the fact that we're a visible reminder of the Mash-Up. Seeing Mashies on TV is one thing. They can imagine that a dog man is just playing a character;

he's not a real person. But seeing us in real life? It brings back some difficult memories for people. That day wasn't a body *swap,* after all. People didn't simply switch seats. Half the people fully *poofed.* Gone. The city was silenced by half.

When one body disappeared, it left a space formerly occupied by someone who was in the middle of something; some of those things were very important. Moving vehicles lost their drivers. Open flames went unattended. Planes lost pilots. People *died* that day.

So, when some people see me, they don't see a girl making coffee; to them, I'm a reminder of how they were hurt and what they lost. Seeing a Mashie says to them that they were never as safe as they thought they were, and they never will be.

"Hey, time to scoot," Sarah says as she bumps me with her hip. "Move so I can clock in."

I shake myself out of my thoughts. What a time to be focusing on sad stuff. I have a date! No moping around allowed.

Besides, my shift is over—time to go shopping.

I check my phone as soon as I'm off and see that Liam texted me. After smiling and squeezing my phone happily for a couple of seconds, I send a reply.

> **Me**: I'm great. Getting off work and running to the store now. What's your favorite color?

I wait a minute to see if he replies, but he must be busy, so I head to the mall instead. Normally I prefer to shop online and then just take things to the tailor to get fitted around my tail, but I don't have time for that today. On the way, I listen to upbeat music and prepare myself for all of the inevitable stares and whispers I'll receive from people around me. I wish I could say it might not happen, but I would be lying if I did.

Thankfully, it's not too busy at the mall early on a weekday. I head to one of the department stores, so I don't have to walk through the whole mall. This entry is in the men's clothing section, so I need to go up a floor, then through the cosmetics to get to the cocktail dresses. There are some subtle double-takes from curious people as I pass them by, but thankfully, no one is too rude.

I make it to the area where the nice dresses are and look through the racks. I check a price tag and bite my lip. Perhaps I should have gone to a less expensive store. My job pays not much more than minimum wage, and these dresses are not cheap. They're so, so pretty, though.

My phone vibrates once quickly in my pocket. It's a text from Liam.

Liam: Red. Why?

Me: Nothing. You'll see. Bye!

Liam: So mean!

I smile as I tuck my phone back into my pocket. Okay, he's definitely worth splurging on a fancy dress. I reach for the sparkly red mini dress in front of me, but a haughty voice stops me.

"Excuse me. I'm going to need you to step away from the clothes, please."

My smile disappears as I turn around and see a gray-haired woman in a severe black suit standing in front of a large man.

"What? Are you talking to me?"

I look around me, confused. They couldn't mean me; I didn't do anything wrong.

"Ma'am, I'm going to need you to empty your pockets right now and return whatever you put into them," says the large, bald man.

My eyebrows shoot straight up in surprise. *What the hell?*

"I didn't take anything! The only thing I put into my pockets was my phone."

I take out my phone to show them, revealing the rest of my pockets as empty afterward. I even open my purse before they can ask and show them that I have nothing in there.

"See? I didn't take anything."

The man and woman look at each other. When the woman's face returns to mine, her lip curls in distaste.

"Perhaps not yet. But who knows what else your kind is up to. You'll have to leave. Please follow Mr. Jones out into the mall."

The man lumbers toward the mall exit, waving to me to come along with him, but I shake my head.

"I'm parked in front of the downstairs exit where the men's clothes are. I'll leave that way."

The woman pulls a walkie-talkie off a clip on her belt and holds it up, though she doesn't use it.

"If you don't leave through the mall exit right now, I'm calling security to take you out. I won't have you Deviants trampling through my goods with your hooves. Now go."

"I don't have hooves," is all I can manage to say as anger and embarrassment boil inside me.

I follow the man out into the mall, doing everything I can to hold my tears inside. I can't cry or yell or resist because someone could film it and use it against my whole kind. I can just imagine the caption now, "Dangerous Mashie Rages in Capital City Mall!" The Separate Species Party would use it as an example of why I shouldn't have rights or something. People will watch it without context, and they won't question it. I'll be the crazy goat Mashie at the mall forever.

For my sake, and for all Mashies, I have to be a perfect example in public at all times. All of us do. It's not right, and it's not fair, and some days I want to just scream and scream and never stop.

Instead, I go into a more affordable shop with a teenage employee who doesn't even look at me twice, and buy a sexy, little, red dress. My face is calm. I even manage half a smile when I thank the apathetic employee for unlocking the dressing room for me so that I can try on the dress. I leave out the side mall entrance to avoid the growing crowd at the main one.

I drive to a side street and sit in my old, beat-up car, and I cry until my tears dry up. When I get myself together, I go to my favorite tailor—who happens to be a cat Mashie—and get the dress fitted around my tail. Then, I go home and put a soothing mask around my eyes to eliminate the puffiness from crying. I can't look bad for my date.

Chapter Eleven

Liam

Tonight's the night. I've never been more excited. My car has been parked around the block from her apartment for half an hour already because I couldn't stand waiting around my house any longer. *Fuck,* I've got it bad, and I'm not even afraid to admit it.

Okay, make sure you look alright. I know I do, but I have to check again. I look in the rear-view mirror and make sure there's nothing in my teeth or nose or on my face and that my hair is smooth. Everything is fine. I check my phone for the millionth time and see it's five minutes to seven. Time to go!

When I get there, I don't have to wait at all. Jill walks right out the door of her ancient, brick building as soon as she sees me pull up.

All the breath shoots out of my lungs at once, the instant I see her.

She's wearing this little red dress. I'm not good at fashion terms or whatever, but the neckline is just low enough to show a little cleavage—and it's damn fine cleavage, too. The dress is pretty form-fitting and shows how she's bouncy in the best places. There is this little flouncy ruffle at the bottom that shows off how thick her thighs are.

Fuck, I want those thighs squeezing my head immediately.

She waves to me, showcasing her adorably dimpled smile. As I wave back with one hand, I discreetly adjust my half-hard cock with the other.

When she opens the car door and turns to scoot into the seat, I see that the dress has been adjusted to make room for her little tail. It pokes out a special hole in the back, wiggling away. Something about that is *so fucking hot.*

Oh no, I was so distracted by how pretty she is that I forgot to get out and open the door like a gentleman. *Shit.*

"Hi, Liam!" she says brightly as she gets comfy in the passenger seat.

"Hi Jill! I'm so sorry I didn't get out and open the door. I don't know what I was thinking. I'm so—"

"Hey, stop. It's okay," Jill interrupts, giggling. "It was faster for me to just get in. I'm hungry, so let's go! A girl's gotta eat!"

She playfully slaps my thigh, and my heart leaps out of my chest and dances across the dashboard. *Get back here, heart! We have stuff to do!*

"Yeah, I'm pretty hungry too. I got us reservations at Rayna's on Fourth. The owner knows my dad, so we should get in pretty fast."

I start the car as soon as her seatbelt clicks and head toward Rayna's. It's a bit of a show-off of a place to be taking her, I'll admit it. I could have taken her anywhere, but I know how hard it is to get into that restaurant and how good it's supposed to be, so I couldn't resist using my connections this time.

"Whoa, you got us into Rayna's? That's awesome! I've never been there. Ah! I'm so excited!"

She drums her hands a few times on the dashboard and bounces in her seat. *Please, please bounce on my cock next. I will do literally anything.*

"Yeah, it's whatever. I've actually never been there, though, so I'm pretty hyped to try it, too. I'm big on dessert, and I hear theirs are damn good."

Out of the corner of my eye, I see Jill arch a brow at me.

"Oh, surprise, you're into sweets. I never would have guessed that Mister Fruity Drinks liked dessert best."

I look over at her quickly to see the cheeky smirk on her face.

"Hey now, we both know I like sweet things, yeah. I mean, I'm on a date with you, right? Can't get much sweeter than that."

I toss a quick smile at her before turning into the restaurant's valet.

"That was so corny," she chuckles. "But please don't stop the compliments, I can take as many as you can give."

"Oh, if you're asking me to compliment you every time I notice something I like about you, I'll never shut up, so be careful what you wish for."

As I pull up to the valet, we're both laughing at my cheesy flirting. I'm glad she's receptive to my attempts, though. *God, she's so sweet.*

We get the car business settled and enter the restaurant. I've been to a lot of nice places. My family is...well, we're more than comfortable financially. But Rayna's is really top tier. The place just screams class. There's nothing trendy or kitschy or experimental about it. It's just classic. Dim lighting, white tablecloths, nothing to show off, but something in the air of the place lets you know that if you're there, you're fucking lucky.

When the maître d notices me, we're escorted right away to a quiet table, no waiting at all. He smiles and hurries; it seems almost as if he wants to bow like I'm some kind of royalty. Most people don't recognize me—my dad purposely distanced himself from me so I wouldn't get hurt by his enemies—but they know who I am here.

As we're walking to our spot, Jill raises her eyebrows at me as if to say she's impressed by how quickly we moved past the line. She's only surprised because I haven't told her about my family yet. If she knew where I came from, she wouldn't be surprised at all. I don't like talking about it, though, at least not until I know people won't use me or try to abuse my friendship. Not after what happened with my ex.

We get to the table and take our seats. Sitting across from me in the candlelight, her face glows golden in the soft lighting. With her goat features against that pitch-black hair, highlighted with fiery light, she could be an ancient goddess come to life.

I feel like I can barely breathe in her presence.

"Liam, did you hear me?" she asks.

I snap to attention. I must have been too distracted to hear what she said.

"I didn't. Can you say it again? Sorry."

I clear my throat and focus intently on her words, trying not to get distracted by the perfect pillows of her lips that are speaking those very words, making sure I don't miss our conversation anymore.

"Oh, I just asked if you have any food allergies. I mean, it's a weird question, I guess. I'm just curious."

Her ears fold backward a little, and I have to stop myself from saying "Aww," because of how cute it is.

"No, I don't. Do you?"

"Pineapple. That's it. Kind of a weird thing to be allergic to, but yeah." Her nose crinkles adorably as she gives a small huff of a laugh.

"I'll make sure I never make us piña coladas then. I swear." I place my hand on my heart.

"Thank you, that means so much. I was so worried about that. Just crippling piña anxiety. I check my closet for them before bed every night, just in case."

We both smile at each other as the waiter comes to the table to take our wine order. Both of us decline wine and only want to drink water. We order our food and wait for it to be delivered.

"So, tell me what you like to do in your free time," I ask before taking a drink of my water. *Somehow, even the water here tastes better than everywhere else. Maybe they have a secret flavor-influencing Superhero. That would be wild, but stranger things have happened.*

"I don't have a ton of free time, to be honest. I work as much as I can to save up. I'm going to get a farm again one day, and I need the money. But in the little bit of downtime I do have, I like to work in the community garden on my block, and I like to game."

"A gamer girl? Nice!" I grin at that. Something we could enjoy doing together, perhaps? "What do you like playing? Anything I'd know?"

"Oh, lots of stuff. Lately, I've been super into Killwatch. I know it's a stupid shooting game or whatever, but it just lets me blow off some steam."

She blushes and shakes her head a little in embarrassment. I, on the other hand, am nearly vibrating with excitement.

"Holy shit, that's my favorite game. I play it every day. Well, used to play it with Frank, but then he was a fucking dick, and I stopped, and now I don't have anyone to play with, and it's not as fun. We can play together, if you want. That would be sick."

I'm a quarter-century-old and practically bouncing in my seat with excitement over finding a new person to play video games with. Fuck it, I don't care if I seem like a child. I'm happy as hell.

"I'd like that," she says with a laugh. "I play tank, though, and I play aggressively."

"Perfect. I'm an idiot of a DPS. We can suck ass as a team together. I don't even care. I'm just excited to play with you."

"I'll play whatever you want, Liam. I'm tired of playing with myself," she says before taking a long sip of her water.

I could swear she said it in a way that meant a lot more than playing video games. *Holy shit.*

"Oh yeah?" I start. I'll be careful, just in case she meant it innocently, but *hot damn,* who says *play with myself* to a date innocently? I have to see if my instinct was correct. "Whatever I want, huh?"

She raises an eyebrow, a smirk on her lips. *Fuck yeah.* She opens her mouth to speak, but just then, the waiter arrives with our food. *Son of a bitch.* I've never been so sad to see a steak in my life.

She claps her hands together as her pasta is set in front of her, and she shimmies in her seat happily. She inhales the garlic and basil scent of her pasta and sighs.

"Oh, this looks so good!" she tells me with a smile.

"Yeah, you do," I say before I can stop myself.

Liam, you corny idiot with the moves of a teenager, shut the fuck up.

She snorts out a laugh as she twirls the pasta on her fork.

"That was so bad. Like, so bad. But thank you."

Her cheeks turn pink, and her strange eyes turn shyly downward.

"It's true. You look incredible. I mean, you always do. It's just that dress really looks fantastic on you."

Her face manages to turn even pinker as she swallows her food. I realize I haven't even started eating, so I grab my knife and fork and dig in. *So tender. So juicy. Absolute perfection.*

"Thank you. I'm lucky I found it. I tried to go to a different place to buy one, but they told me to leave because I'm..." She points to her horns. "Yeah. I didn't want to risk that happening again, so I had to go to a shop that was friendly to Mashies and hope they had something. Thankfully, they had this cute dress!"

She smiles at the end of her story, but I can see there is a lingering sadness, and even anger, about what happened at the first store. I know I'm sure as shit angry.

"They kicked you out?" I grip my knife so hard my knuckles turn white. "Just because you're a Mashie? That's fucked up. What place? And who was it?"

Whoever it was is getting their ass fired. If I can use my family's influence to make worse happen, I will too. How *the fuck* can they treat her like that?

"Liam, relax. It happens more often than you'd think. You can't get that mad every time something happens, or you'll *never* calm down."

I shake my head. "No, no way. You can't be so relaxed about this. If you let them get away with it, they'll just do it again. Tell me who it is, and I'll have them fired *tonight*."

I can see her jaw clench, and I start to worry that maybe I've made a misstep here.

"If they get fired over this, it's *Mashies* that they'll hate even more. They'll blame *us*, not you. They'll spread even more hate."

"So you're doing nothing? You can't just let them get away with treating you like that."

"You think I want to?" She springs up, leaning forward now, both hands flat on the table.

Yeah, I fucked up.

"You think it feels good not knowing what to do because every option leaves me and those like me fucked worse than before? You have *no clue* what this is like, Liam. *None.*"

"I just want to help. It's not fair that they did that. That's all."

"A lot of things aren't fair. Look, I don't know much about you, but from what I've seen tonight, it's clear you have a lot of privilege, so maybe you don't know that." She picks up the few things she brought and shakes her head. "I don't know if we're going to be able to understand one another, Liam. You seem nice, but I don't have it in me to explain what real pain is to someone who's never felt it. So, this isn't going to work. Thank you, though; you were very sweet."

My mouth hangs open as she gets up and walks to the door. *Did that just happen? Did I fumble that bad?* I shake my head, then stand up, following Jill. As I pass the waiter, I tell him to put it on my dad's account and to give himself a large tip. He seems fine with that. When I make it out the door, I see Jill pull out her phone, presumably to call a ride.

"Jill, please," I beg. "Let me talk to you. I really need to. Please."

She looks down at her phone, then back at me, before nodding. She slides the phone back into her purse and crosses her arms. I have the valet bring my car around, and we get in. I drive us to the next block, where I pull over on a quiet street.

"Is it ok if we stop here to talk? I need to get this shit out."

"Yeah, that's fine," she replies, fussing with the hem of her skirt, not looking at me.

"Ok. Well, I know pain. Let me tell you what happened with Jennifer."

Chapter Twelve

Liam

I STARTED DATING JENNIFER when I was in eighth grade. I was kind of a geek. This scrawny, lanky dork who was just way too interested in bugs. But she liked me, even though she was pretty and smart and popular.

We became a real couple. I mean, we were just kids, but we were together every year of high school and college. We lost our virginities together. Everything. I did everything she asked of me. Everything she wanted, even when I didn't want to. I was happy as long as she was happy.

When we were twenty, I asked her to marry me. She said yes. I was so fucking happy. This gorgeous, "perfect" woman was going to be my wife. I thought we had a romance like no other. It was great. And then the Mash-Up happened.

Jennifer and I got mashed together. We were in her body, not mine. Let me just say, it's fucking weird and awful being mashed with someone and being the invisible part.

Then the government found a fix through Honor Man and started separating people. Well, Jennifer and I were one of the last two to be separated.

She had been kind of weird the whole time we'd been stuck together, but I figured it was just because of the situation. I didn't expect anything shady. I was so wrong. I found out when we went to a grocery store we didn't normally go to.

Some prick came up to her, calling her name. She was ignoring him. I was confused, like, this strange guy knows her, so why isn't she acknowledging him? But then, when he got closer, he wrapped his arms around her and planted a kiss right on her fucking mouth.

He says to her, "I'm glad to see you, mi amor. I have missed speaking to you. Did you get the alimony yet? Or did you not marry the little prince?"

My mind was spinning in confusion. I'd never seen this guy in my life, but he's kissing my fiancée and talking nonsense now. I tried to open her mouth to speak, but Jennifer got there first.

"I'm sorry, sir, I don't know what you're talking about," she told him and began to walk away.

"Ah, you must still have a Rider inside you. Many apologies, Jennifer," the man said with a tip of his hat as he backed away. As soon as her body relaxed enough for me to speak, I did.

"Jen, I think you need to explain what just happened," I ground out from her mouth.

She was silent for a moment before nodding, then heading toward the door, setting our half-full basket of groceries on the customer service desk on the way out.

When we got outside, Jennifer didn't go to the car. She walked down the block to a public park and sat on a bench. There weren't a lot of people around, but enough that if something strange happened, they would notice. I knew Jen well enough to know she did that on purpose.

She didn't want me to make a scene, and she was about to tell me something big.

"Before the Mash-Up, I was seeing that man. I've seen other men, too. I plan to see more." She stated it very matter-of-factly, as if she were talking about the fucking weather, not ripping my heart open.

"He said something about getting alimony, being married. What did that mean, Jen?" Tears built up in her eyes, from my heartbreak.

She sighed. "I was going to marry you long enough to get alimony, then get divorced. After that, go do whatever I want, I suppose."

If it were only me in that body, it would have been a blubbering mess, but as I was barely controlling a shred of it, only a single tear fell to show my unfathomable level of torment.

"After all this time? How could you? I love you. What did I do wrong?"

"Nothing. I just don't love you like that anymore. I haven't for a long time, but I didn't know how to tell you. You just...you have so much money, and influence, and you don't do anything with it. I kept thinking of all the things I wanted to do, but I couldn't do any of it if I were to leave you and lose access to your money. So, when I met Rocco, and he told me to marry you and take some in the divorce, it made perfect sense."

She was still so cold about it. She was nothing like the girl I thought she was, just sitting there, hands in her lap, casually watching the cars go past.

"If you wanted money, you could have asked for it. Even if you left me. If you really knew me, you'd know that. Fuck you, Jen. You wrecked everything, you got nothing, and you broke my heart. How does it feel?"

She tilted her head as if to consider my question before replying. "You're wrong. I don't have nothing. I have youth, education, and beauty. I have control of this body. I'll be just fine, Liam. Right now, you're the one with nothing. Until we get separated, you don't exist. So, you'd better watch your tone with me."

We were both quiet as we sat and watched the cars go by for several more minutes. I've never been more frightened. She could have pushed me down inside of her, and to the world, I'd be gone. I'd have to silently watch everything she did for the rest of her life. I had no control over anything.

I finally broke the silence. "Let's go home."

She didn't reply, just stood up, and took us to the car to drive us back to my house.

We did get separated, but it wasn't right away. Like I said, we were some of the very last people on the list. I spent weeks inside her, terrified I'd never get out. I had to listen to her talk to men, tell them how she was going to fuck them, keeping silent while my soul felt crushed.

The fear and the pain were indescribable. Afterward, I didn't think I'd ever get over it. I definitely didn't think I'd ever find someone who could make my heart feel fucking alive again.

That is, until I walked into a coffee shop and saw a beautiful woman behind the counter. So beautiful, I couldn't even speak.

"Jill," I whisper her name like a prayer, a plea, "you have made me feel like I can breathe again. Don't go. I may not understand what you're going through, but I know pain. And I want to know *you*, all the good and bad."

Chapter Thirteen

Jill

Well, I feel like an asshole.

After a moment of silence, I turn to look at Liam. He's staring out the spotless windshield, his face devoid of expression, eyes limned in the silver of moonlight.

"I'm sorry. I shouldn't have assumed," I say as I tentatively lay my hand on his shoulder.

He lost his jacket at some point, probably at the restaurant. I hope he gets it back. It's a nice jacket.

His eyes soften, lips turning up ever so slightly when he turns to look at me.

"It's fine. I can see why you'd think I have everything easy compared to you. Just easy in life in general. And I'm sorry too. I admit I don't know what you're going through or how things should be handled. I'm just tired of not being able to help in the world, and I reacted too quickly. That's why I'm working with Sir Cicada, though—to help. We're working to split those who weren't able to be separated after the Mash-Up. Maybe if we can do that, I won't have such a Hero complex." He laughs weakly.

I smile in return. He really is a sweetheart. I like that he's self-aware and willing to apologize when he's wrong and willing to forgive me when I am. Something is bothering me a little, and I need to ask about it, though.

"Hey, why do you keep mentioning how easy you have it, who your dad is, all that? Is this something I should know? I feel like I've been left out of some important information or something."

He shifts in his seat and looks away from me. His hands tighten on the steering wheel as if he'd like to drive away from this topic.

"Yeah, I don't exactly advertise it—and he *really* doesn't—but my dad is Honor Man. Ugh, I hate calling him that. Anyway, we've been rich my whole life, because he used his powers secretly for profit before Superheroes came out to the public. It's kind of an open secret among Heroes that they assisted the ultra-wealthy and the government before the Mash-Up revealed them to the public, but whatever. He didn't like people knowing I was his kid because I don't have any powers, and he was afraid I would get hurt. So, yeah. That's me, the powerless and unknown son of the most powerful and well-known man in the world."

We sit in another moment of silence. I pull my hand away and flop my whole body back heavily into the seat.

"Fucking hell, I can't even escape Honor Man on a date," I complain. "On the news all day and night, face plastered everywhere, people won't stop talking about him. Now the guy I like is related to him. I'm cursed."

Liam chokes out a laugh but quickly tries to quiet himself.

"Jill, that's my dad. I should really defend him. I'm just happy you said you like me, though."

He breaks out into full-on riotous laughter. I join in. He's so cute when he laughs. He looks so boyish and carefree. It makes me want to kiss him. So I do.

It's quick. I just lean over, put my hand on his cheek to still him, and plant a quick, soft kiss on his warm lips. His eyes widen in surprise, and he takes a sharp breath.

"I did not expect that," he says before even exhaling.

"Sorry." I blush. "You just look so cute when you laugh."

He breaks out in a wide grin.

"I should laugh more, then."

"You should. But I think I'd like to kiss you more, whether or not you do. You're very kissable."

My face feels about a thousand degrees now. Why am I so shy about kissing? I'm acting like a teenager!

"We could go to my apartment. It would probably be way better for kissing than sitting in the car in front of a doggy daycare," he says with a chuckle.

"Hey, what kind of girl do you think I am?" I ask with an exaggeratedly affronted expression.

His jaw drops, and his eyes fly open in a horrified look, and I realize he thinks I'm serious.

"No, no, I'm kidding. I'm not offended. I'd like to go back to your apartment, but I want to play Killwatch. Is that a deal?"

I hold out my hand, and he grins again before taking hold of it and giving it a good shake.

"Deal. Let's see how good a tank you are."

Chapter Fourteen

Liam

She's a damn good tank.

When we got to my apartment, she used the restroom while I made some popcorn and grabbed us some sodas. After that, we sat down in the living room on the sofa and started up the game. It didn't take long for me to realize she is much, much better than I am, but thankfully, she carried the fuck out of me.

"GG EZ, bitch," she yells into the mic.

We just had a match where one of the players had been brutally sexist to her. She absolutely annihilated him. *Fuck*, it was hot.

"Jill, you're going to get us banned," I admonish, but really only half-heartedly. The guy deserved to be told off.

"Eh, I've been banned before. Never been caught for ban evasion though." She laughs mischievously, and I shake my head with a grin. She's a spicy one.

"Well, I think I might be ready for a break. Do you want something to eat? Or to watch something on TV for a little bit?" I scratch the back of my neck nervously. I've never actually had to date like this before. *Am I doing okay?*

"Are you sure you're not quitting because you can't handle how amazing I am at the game? Or is it that now that you have seen my gamer rage, you're afraid of me? Rawr!" She makes claws with her hands and does a pouncing motion.

"Gamer rage? Afraid?" I bust out laughing.

"I knew I could make you laugh again."

Her eyes drop to my lips, and she turns in her seat so that her hips are better facing mine. My throat bobs with a sudden anxiety. *Oh fuck oh fuck oh fuck oh fuck.*

"You sure did," is all I can manage to get out.

It seems to be enough, though, because her eyes go half lidded, and she leans very slightly toward me. That surely is a sign. My breath is shaky, but I lift a hand to her cheek and go in for the kiss. It's perfect.

Her lips are so incredibly soft and full. Her cheek is hot under my hand. She smells like cinnamon and coffee and motherfucking Pine-Sol. *Ugh, I love the scent of Pine-Sol.*

She pushes her mouth harder against mine, wrapping an arm around my neck, with a soft moan. I grip her waist, tug her to me, and move my other hand from her cheek to the back of her neck, where I can feel the softness of her smooth hair. She slips her tongue against the seam of my lips, and I open my mouth gladly, letting her little tongue explore my mouth before I let mine more aggressively explore hers. She tastes like popcorn and orange soda. She's perfect.

After several minutes of the gradually deepening kiss, she pulls away.

"Wow. That was...wow," she says, still panting.

"Yeah. That pretty much covers it." I chuckle.

"I have to work in the morning. I wish I could stay longer. I should have left already, but we were having so much fun. Now I feel like if I stay any longer, I'll be here all night."

By the way her eyes heat when she says *all night,* I can tell exactly what she means. My cock strains in my pants. I really, really cannot wait to get her alone again.

"When can I see you again?" I ask, twirling one of her soft locks around my finger.

"Can I make you dinner tomorrow night? Here, not my apartment. There's a...weird situation there. Or is that too soon?"

She bites her lip, waiting for an answer.

"Not too soon at all. I can't wait. Let's get you home and get some sleep. Sooner we sleep, the sooner it will be tomorrow."

She grins at me, showing her cute dimple.

"That's what I always say! Alright, sounds good. Let's do it."

Fuck, I can't wait to do it.

Chapter Fifteen

Jill

WORK FEELS LIKE IT takes nine billion years to finish. Seriously, it has never dragged on that long before. Thinking of seeing Liam again tonight has got me all worked up, and I cannot keep my mind on anything else. By the time my shift is over, I'm practically ready to tear my apron to shreds and jump over the counter and never come back.

At the ass crack of dawn, I went to the grocery store to get ingredients to cook for Liam tonight. I thought all night about what to cook for him. Nothing that takes too long, nothing too messy, but nothing so easy that I don't impress him at least a little. Something he might not expect.

After a bit of thinking, I decided to make him barbacoa lengua tacos. I know it doesn't seem like an obvious choice, but I was able to do a major part of the cooking in the slow cooker while I was at work, which means more time for hanging out and less time at the stove at his house. And I get to bring him something he probably doesn't get to have every day. For dessert, I'll make matcha cream puffs to show off my pastry-making skills. I learned the dinner recipe growing up from my mom and the dessert recipe from my aunt on my dad's side, so it's also a little bit of family luck as a bonus.

Once I got the groceries, I prepared what I needed for the slow cooker, then went to work. Then home to take a shower, dry my hair, and do all the stuff I need to so that I can be prepared for an overnight stay...just in case, of course. Not that I'm planning on it or anything. Maybe just hoping. Really, really hoping.

At seven o'clock on the dot, he shows up at my house to grab me and my grocery bag full of food. We happily greet one another and make the fifteen-minute trip to his house. We make small talk in the car, and even though it's not anything anyone would consider thrilling, my heart is still racing with excitement.

We get to his apartment, and I'm again impressed by how nice it is. As I set up in the kitchen, I can't help but notice how much all the appliances must have cost. Everything is stainless steel, high-tech, and highly polished. Keeping a kitchen like this spotless when he works full-time means he either doesn't use it or he has a cleaning person come in to do it for him. I wonder which it is.

"What are you looking at?" Liam asks from behind me.

He's taller than I am by more than a little, but not so much that I can imagine any sort of positions being difficult between us. Oh...*I'm imagining positions between us.* I clear my throat and focus on his appliances again to cool down my heated cheeks.

Then I realize I've been looking at all his stuff for an awkwardly long time without saying anything.

"Your kitchen is super nice. Your fridge has a screen on the front. What's that for?" I move closer to his refrigerator and touch the screen. It flares to life, and it shows what looks like a video of the inside of a mostly empty fridge.

"Oh, yeah, so it shows what's inside when I touch it, so I don't have to open it to look. It also has a setting that texts me to let me know when I'm out of staple items. I don't know, it does a bunch of stuff. It's pretty cool, I guess. I mostly just eat out, though. Or eat whatever pretty girls bring over for me."

"Oh, you get a lot of pretty girls here?" I raise an eyebrow.

"So many. Just knocking down the door to bring me casseroles and stuff. It's a problem, really." He shakes his head and leans back on the counter as if exhausted.

His perfectly white t-shirt rides up as he bends backward, revealing just the tiniest sliver of firm flesh. *Well, now, that's just torture.*

"Oh, poor you. How will you ever cope?" I put my hands over my heart and lean toward him.

"It's just my curse to bear. Now, what casserole have you brought to punish me with, pretty girl?"

"No casserole, my apologies," I laugh. "I brought barbacoa lengua. Beef tongue."

Grade A, free-range, genetically tested beef tongue. As grim as it is to think about it, you can't be too careful with animal products these days.

"Tongue...is that a hint?"

He smiles playfully, making my cheeks redden all over again. I didn't even think of that.

"If you play your cards right, perhaps," I reply, trying to sound as if I knew what I was doing all along.

It seems to succeed because his eyes go straight to my mouth. They darken enough to let me know exactly in what direction his thoughts are headed.

I clear my throat and turn around to begin preparing the food. Eat first, then figure out what happens after that. Eat the lengua, then decide what to do with the tongue.

Chapter Sixteen

Liam

SHE SHOOS ME OUT of the kitchen after a couple of minutes when she says I'm distracting her, so I go to the dining room to make sure everything is set up, then play some games for a bit until she tells me everything is ready. She serves all the food, steaming hot and fragrant. I squeeze lime on top, then take my first bite.

"Holy shit, this is fantastic," I say around a mouthful of meat and tortilla.

Lime is one of my favorite flavors, so getting it for dinner is a treat. I swallow it down and chase it with a drink of the beer she brought, which pairs perfectly.

"You can really cook!"

"Aw, thanks." She blushes, and it's so cute I could just pinch her cheeks. "Now, keep eating. I brought dessert too."

I gladly take another big bite. I watch her eat as I do, and when she drips a little onto her cleavage, I nearly die watching her wipe it off. I think I glance at her cleavage ten times in the next five minutes after that, while thinking about licking it.

"So, tell me, what kinds of things did you do for fun before the Mash-Up? Did things change after?" she asks.

"I mean, to be honest, I was kind of controlled by Jennifer for years; I just was blind to it. Like, I really liked playing video games since I was a teen, but when she would find out I was playing them on a school night, she'd throw a shit fit. She'd say I was ruining my future by not studying or doing other things that could benefit my education or future career options. Stuff like that. We mostly did stuff she liked when we did go out, like watched polo matches or went to parties at the homes of other kids who...well, to be straight up, other kids with money. When she was gone, I was kind of lost. Didn't know what I liked. Sometimes I still feel like I'm learning." I huff out a single laugh. "I do know. I like to play Killwatch, I like researching stuff related to bugs, and I like spending time with you."

"I'm sorry you had to deal with her. She's a fucking abusive piece of shit, and I'm glad she's out of your life." She reaches over and rubs the back of my hand. "I promise I'll never treat you like that, okay?"

"I believe you. And same to you. I hope no one has ever treated you like that." I say it as a statement, but it's kind of a question. I know this is serious talk territory but might as well get it out of the way.

"No, thankfully. I mean, it's not like every re-lationship was great, but nothing I would consider abusive. I haven't dated a lot; my last relationship was pretty long-term, and so was the one before that. My last was really kind to me, but when the Mash-Up hap-pened just couldn't handle my mental health deterio-rating the way it did, and honestly, I can't blame him." She chews on her thumbnail absently, a faraway look on her face.

"That's kind of crappy that he couldn't hang just because you got sick for a while." I take her hand and hold it. She looks at me, her eyes focusing on the here and now again.

"No, really, I understand. I wasn't myself back then. I got so depressed I couldn't function, couldn't do anything to the point I lost the farm, the thing I cared most about in the world. I was that bad. He had his own issues to deal with, and the two of us just didn't work. It just goes like that sometimes." There's a pause before she cocks her head. "You've never dated a Mashie, right?"

"No, no, I don't even know any except you. Which probably sounds bad, but I swear it's just a circumstance thing and not like I'm avoiding Mashies or anything." I grimace.

She laughs and squeezes my hand.

"It's ok. I was just wondering if there were going to be awkward questions or something, and I wanted to get ahead of them. I'll tell you right now that I'm human under my clothes, ok? So, don't think there's going to be anything weird going on. People always want to know about that, so there's your answer." Now her face turns *really* bright red, and so does mine.

"Good to know, uh, thanks." I chuckle.

We're both awkwardly quiet for a minute, not looking at each other, sitting over our empty china plates.

"OK, so you're done eating. How about we have dessert?" She breaks the silence.

"Sounds fantastic!"

We get up and walk to the kitchen, where she leads me to the counter. She turns around to tell me something when suddenly her face opens in an expression of pain.

Chapter Seventeen

Jill

"Ouch!" I exclaim as my stupid tail gets stubbed against the counter.

"Whoa, what's wrong?" Liam asks, stepping backward, brow furrowed in concern.

"I just bonked my tail on the counter. It always gets in the way. It's embarrassing."

"Nope, it's an opportunity," he says with a raised eyebrow and a grin.

I raise my eyebrow in return.

"Say what?"

"An opportunity to lift you onto the kitchen island and use that as an excuse to hold you," he says right before doing exactly that.

I yelp as he scoops me up, holding me against him as he whirls around to face the marble island in the center of his kitchen. He sets me gently down on top of it, careful not to jam my tail.

"Is that better?" he asks, his voice suddenly gone soft.

At this height, I can see straight into his eyes, the crystal blue of them, and I could feel trapped in that ice forever. I'd welcome it, too.

"Much better."

His hands land on my waist, gliding up and down in short strokes. His eyes fall to my cleavage again. This time, I don't let it slide. I grab one of his hands and drag it up my body until it's over my breast, his thumb lying right between the cleavage he was so enamored with at dinner. His breath catches, and he walks closer yet to the island, forcing me to spread my legs to let him in.

"Jill, you're going to drive me crazy," he rasps directly against my neck.

Liam rubs his thumb over the spot on my shirt covering my nipple, and even through the layers of fabric, it feels so, so good. He drags his teeth gently down my neck, and I can't stop my hips from arching upward.

"Oh, Liam, kiss me," I beg.

He obliges me, kissing me hard and deeply. I've never been kissed like this, like I'm being eaten alive *in the best way possible,* and I could do this forever.

But he breaks the kiss and moves his lips down my neck instead, kissing and licking there. It feels so good, I can't help but grab his hair and hold him tight.

"You taste so good," he moans as he works his way from my neck to my chest.

I can't even reply with words. All that comes out is something between a squeak and a moan as he tugs down my shirt, then slides down each cup of my pink lace bra, exposing my breasts to the warm air. He pulls his head back for a second and looks with an appreciative groan before taking one nipple into his mouth and gently sucking.

"Liam, Liam," I repeat over and over as I run my fingers through his hair.

He licks and sucks on each one in turn, turning me into an aching mess between the legs. Each time he glances up into my eyes, I feel like a goddess up here on a throne. And yet I want *more*. I wouldn't dare ask for it. I don't have to, though, because he gives it.

"Taste so good. You're perfect, Jill," he whispers as he unbuttons my pants.

When they're unbuttoned, he fumbles a little at the back with how to slide them off my tail. Once that's done, he does manage to get them off my hips and down my legs, along with my panties. I feel incredibly exposed without pants and with my breasts out, while he's fully dressed, but the bulge in his pants and the way his pupils are fully blown out show that his appreciation of my form might even outweigh my shyness.

Liam drops down so that his face is level with my hips, and I inhale sharply. *Eep.*

"Slide forward. All the way to the edge," he commands, voice rough.

"Yes, sir," I reply, trying to joke, but the sound comes out far too serious, and I see his eyes flash at the word *sir*.

I think someone may have a budding kink to explore. I swallow hard and slide to the edge of the island. Though I'm cringing inside, I spread my legs wide before him.

"Fuck, Jill," he groans before kissing a line from the inside of my knee up my inner thigh.

At the first graze of his lips against my cunt I nearly arch off the surface of the island. Liam grabs my hips and holds me firmly down. He looks absolutely feral as he begins to lick me greedily, like a starved lion tearing into the body of an antelope. When I whimper, and he snaps those blue eyes up to mine, the feeling of being *prey* only increases. And it feels *so good*.

Liam sucks on my clit, and the sensation is so overwhelming I can't help but push backward to escape the feeling. It's not intentional; I certainly don't want to stop. My body just decided to betray me.

Liam pulls me back to the edge.

"Where do you think you're going?" he asks, and his voice sounds darker, smokier. If I weren't already dripping wet, I would be now.

"It just felt so good. I got overwhelmed. Sorry."

He drags his teeth along the inside of my thigh until he's almost to my center again.

"Don't go anywhere again until I'm finished. You're going to come on my face so I can taste what a sweet, perfect girl you are. Then I'm going to take you to my bedroom and make you come as many more times as you'd like, but this one, this one is mine. Now, let me taste you."

All I can do is nod and open my legs wider as he goes back to work on me, this time inserting two fingers into my throbbing pussy as well. It doesn't take long before he's curling his fingers and sucking my clit, and I'm shouting his name to the high, bright, very expensive lighting.

I feel like I'm made of gelatin; I want to lie back and sleep, but that's not going to happen. Liam wraps my legs around his waist and my arms around his shoulders and lifts me, carrying me out of the kitchen and across the apartment.

Is he really taking me to his bedroom?

"Where are we going?" I ask as I run my fingers through his silky hair.

"We're going to have a lot of fun," he says as he picks up speed, jogging down a hall lined with exotic wood floors.

Chapter Eighteen

Liam

We make it to my room in no time flat. My bed is pretty big and has soft, black sheets. It just feels so nice, I don't know. I hope she doesn't expect some massive thing with, like, red silk sheets or something. I just barely stop myself from laughing at the thought as I lay her carefully down. I make sure to lay her on her side and not her back because I don't want to smash her tail. I slide next to her, and we lie nose to nose.

"Hey," she whispers, stroking my hair as I place my hand on her hip.

"Hey, to you. Did you know you're in my bed? That's weird."

"What? I am?" She makes an exaggerated, shocked face. "What are we going to do in this totally strange situation I wasn't at all aware we were in?"

We both break out in giggles, and I run my hands up her body until my hand cups her cheek.

"What would you like to do? I mean, I can think of a million things. Like so many things. But maybe you should tell me what you'd be comfortable with," I say before planting a gentle kiss on her lips.

"Well, first, I feel weird being undressed while you're fully clothed, so either I need my pants back, or you have to take off yours. Up to you." She shrugs and bites her bottom lip.

"Uh, that's not a difficult decision," I say as I roll over flat on my back, reaching down to grab the hem of my shirt and then pulling it up over my head.

I keep myself in shape using the gym that's one of this building's amenities, so I know I look at least okay. My stomach is flat and pretty toned. I'm no fitness model or anything, but I'm pretty confident. Jill runs a finger across my stomach, and I flex involuntarily, exhaling abruptly. She hums approvingly. *Score.* She lifts her shirt off as well, as it was only half off before. She is now fully nude before me. My mind goes absolutely dead for a moment before she shoves me on the shoulder.

"Pants, still on," she says with a laugh.

"Oh, yeah, I forgot about me. Anyone would with you in the room."

I slide off my bottom clothes, letting my cock spring free. I've been hard most of the time she's been here, so it feels pretty good not to be trapped in those pants.

"Mmm, now that looks delicious," she purrs, licking her lips as her eyes devour me.

"What do you mean?" I rasp out, knowing very well what she means.

Jill runs a hand flat down my stomach as she angles her body further toward me. She slides down slowly, laying a soft kiss on my shoulder, then another on my chest.

"I mean," she says before kissing my stomach, "I want to know if I'll find you as delicious as you found me."

She kisses my hip bone before looking into my eyes. "Can I taste you, Liam?'

"Fuck yes," I choke out. Not the most eloquent response, but I'm lucky I can say anything at this point.

Jill slips one leg between my thighs, followed by the second. She sits up until she kneels, and I sit up until we're face to face. I wrap my arms around her, taking her mouth in a deep, wet kiss. She slides a hand between us until she meets my cock, wrapping her hand around it to slowly stroke up and down. I groan into her mouth. She pushes my chest away with her other hand.

"Lay back, okay?"

I sink back into the feather pillows, barely feeling their softness with my body, hyper-focused on the feel of her smooth hands. One grips my hip as she lowers herself, the second circles the base of my shaft. When her mouth is a hair's breadth away from the head of my cock she pauses, looks up at me with those golden eyes, and winks, before opening wide and taking me in all the way down to meet her closed fist.

My hips rise to meet her as I hiss out my pleasure. She begins a routine—a twisting stroke, a soft, wet sucking, punctuated with harder sucks. Her cheeks hollow as she goes deep enough to pass the back of her throat. Her tongue flicks and glides and circles all the best places. Her opposite hand massages my balls until the point when I'm almost ready to come. But I stop her.

I stop her hand, gently grab both sides of her face, and lift her off of me. I sit us up until we're face-to-face once again.

"Jill. Do you want to..." I don't know why I'm shy all of a sudden. I just had my face on her cunt and my cock in her mouth, but for some reason, this feels different. "I mean, I want to, you know, with you, and I'm wondering if you want to too."

"Want to what?" Jill cocks her head to the side as if she doesn't understand, but there's a sparkle in those square pupils that tells me she knows damn well what I mean.

"You know..." I roll my eyes and huff out a small laugh.

"Maybe I do, maybe I don't." She straddles my lap, and I can feel how wet her pussy is when it grazes my cock. "But you have to say it. I know you want to take control. I could see it in your eyes earlier. In fact, I think you need to be the one in control for once. So I want you to tell me *exactly* what you want. Be explicit."

The thought of her doing whatever I want right now, willingly, enthusiastically, makes me nearly come right then. *I guess she has a point.* Her dark hair falls forward as she leans in, only a kiss away from my face. She runs one finger along my jawline and down my neck.

In a husky voice, she begs: "Tell me what you want. Please, *Sir*, I'm yours."

Annnnd that settles it. I scramble to open the drawer on the side table with one hand while I keep the other on her round ass. I bought condoms just in case, thinking I probably wouldn't use them, but having just that glimmer of hope that I might. *Thank you, hope!* I kiss her hard to distract her from my fumbling until I grab hold of one.

"Jill," I rasp out. I clear my throat and say in a much more commanding tone: "Jill, I want to fuck you. Now."

She sits back and smiles wickedly, her horns adding to her devilishly naughty appearance.
"Yes, Sir."

Chapter Nineteen

Jill

"How do you want me?" I run a hand down my chest, drawing his eyes to my breasts.

"First, on top. I want to see those perfect tits bounce. I'm going to make you cum on top of me, under me, next to me, everywhere I can get you. But I need to see your face when you shout my name this time, baby. Get up now."

Liam slides the condom on without any awkwardness. He pulls my hips up until my entrance is positioned directly above his cock.

I take him into my hand and slowly sink. It's been a long time for me, but the lubrication on the condom, my wetness, and our gentle pace help to stretch me out on his big cock without too much discomfort. I let out a loud groan when he's fully sheathed within me, feeling so, so perfectly stuffed.

"That's a good girl," he breathes out. "You take me so well. Your tight pussy stretches so nicely over my thick cock. Now I need you to show me how good you can fuck, alright? Let me see those gorgeous tits while you squeeze that sweet cunt around me. Okay, baby girl?"

Holy fuck. I knew he was holding back, but I didn't realize he'd have such a filthy mouth. *Yes!*

"Yes, Sir," I squeak out as I begin to ride him as smoothly as I can after years out of practice.

It takes a bit to get my rhythm going, and my thighs burn after a while from admittedly being more out of shape than I had realized, but eventually I am solidly fucking him like a pro. The way he's gritting his teeth and gasping for breath as his eyes flit madly between my face, my breasts, and the point where our centers meet tells me he's having a damn good time.

I'm having quite a pleasant time myself, but it gets even better when he starts thrusting up faster into me and circling my clit with his thumb. The sensation at that point becomes entirely overwhelming, and I clench around him, freezing as he fucks up into me through my orgasm.

"Fuck, Liam, yes," I shout, finally beginning to come down enough to move my muscles.

Liam sits up and holds me to him, kissing me hard, still very gently rolling his hips to work himself up and down inside me. I run my hands through his sweaty hair and take in his deliciously musky scent. He pulls away from the kiss and rubs his face along the fur of my ear. I could almost cry with happiness that he isn't disgusted by it if I wasn't so focused on my throbbing cunt at the moment.

"Get on your hands and knees. Let me see your ass in the air," he growls.

I scramble to comply. For a second, I feel self-conscious about my tail, but when he runs his hands over the backs of my thighs, the thickness of my ass cheeks, the wideness of my hips, and moans with desire, I know the view can't be too bad for him. When he adds a soft stroke to the base of my tail, my whole body jerks forward.

"I'm sorry, did that hurt?" he asks.

"No, not at all. It feels good, actually, like a good massage. I just didn't expect it. No one's ever touched it before. Continue."

Liam leans over and places a kiss on the back of my neck, making me shiver. He lines up my hips with his and puts the head of his cock at my entrance. With one hard, slow thrust, he pushes into me, dragging out low moans from both of us.

"Fuck, you feel so good. Perfect." He's seated fully inside me for a moment, hands gripping my hips, before he begins to move again.

For a man who spends his days at a microscope and his nights at a gaming console, he sure moves his hips like a dancer. He rocks and rolls inside me, hitting every spot that needs hitting. When he grazes my G-spot, he sticks with it, reaching across me with one hand to rub at my clit. I come so hard, tears fall from my eyes, and I have to bury my face in the pillow so he doesn't see it and think I'm hurt or something.

And somehow, he's still not done. My body is just absolutely weak at this point, but he lays me on my back, tosses my legs over his shoulders so that my hips are elevated, and my tail isn't smushed, and kisses me while he fucks me hard and fast to his completion. I even come one more time, gently, while he does, just to end things off right.

He turns us on our sides, him big spoon and me the little spoon, careful not to crush my tail. He kisses my shoulder, my neck, my hair, even my horns, which makes tears fall again.

"Was that okay, Jill?" he whispers.

"That was wonderful, Liam."

And it was. It was fantastic. I really like this guy. I'm in deep. *Oh, boy.*

"We never had dessert," he grumbles.

I laugh as I wipe the tears from my cheeks.

"I'll make you dessert for breakfast. I think we'll probably be busy the rest of tonight with round two coming up and all."

He gets up onto one elbow and says in a voice like an excited puppy: "There's going to be a round two?"

"You bet your ass there is."

I hope for many more rounds in the future.

Chapter Twenty

Jill

THERE WAS A ROUND two. And a round three, in the shower the next morning, that made us too far behind in schedule for me to make my dessert for breakfast. He suggested we both take the day off work, but I had to decline. Money is still a problem for me, and that problem isn't fixed by good dick.

When I get home, I rush in, hoping to escape my mom and Uncle Sal's notice before I can slip into my room, but unfortunately, they are in the living room watching some daytime television. A game show with some kind of word guessing and hollering from the audience, the type that keeps you entertained when you're a kid and have a sick day off from school.

"Jillian! There you are. We didn't know if you were alive or dead. You could have called, you know," my mother says, hand on her chest as if her heart is strained.

I roll my eyes and sigh. "You knew exactly where I was. You helped me with the barbacoa while I was at work, for crying out loud."

A sheepish grin appears on her face. She props her chin on the back of the sofa and says, "Alright, you got me. Now tell me what happened! Was he nice to you? Did he like the food?”

“He better have been nice,” Uncle Sal interrupts with her mouth. “I’ll go down there and show him what happens to men who aren’t nice to sweet girls if he wasn’t.”

I imagine my Uncle Sal stomping up to Liam in my mother’s body, flowered dress, pink slippers, and yellow dish gloves on, trying to pick a fight, and I can’t help but snort.

“He was nice, I swear. And yes, he liked the food. We’re going to see each other again very soon. I really, really like him.”

“Aww, I’m glad,” my mother sighs.

“Did you know he’s working on a cure for people like you and Uncle Sal, who are still stuck together? That’s what he’s been doing every day in his research facility. It’s some project with Sir Cicada. He says they’ve made some big breakthroughs lately. I’m not trying to give false hope or anything, he just seemed really certain of it.”

I shove my hands into my back pockets and rock on my feet, waiting for their reaction. It doesn’t take long for my mom to get to her feet and walk over to me, putting her hands on my shoulders.

“That’s wonderful, sweetie. I wish him the best of luck.”

“I’ll tell him that, Mom. Okay, I have to get ready for work, or else I’m gonna be late.” I give my mom a kiss on the cheek and head to my room to get dressed.

The day is uneventful, same old tea and coffee as always. I have a brief text exchange with Liam where he tells me he’s going to have to stay a little late because of the massive breakthrough they’ve just had, and I hide my disappointment. I don't really have anything to do after work, so I head home and lie in bed, scrolling the internet mindlessly.

Hmm. I wonder if he's updated his social media at all.

The thought comes to me, and I can't shake it. I know it's really soon, but *maybe* he's said something about me or us. I tap my nails on my laptop for a moment before inevitably deciding to look him up again. Once I get to his profile, I immediately wish I hadn't.

The first image shared to his profile is of a goat dressed in a bikini with heart emojis all around it. The caption says: "This your girl?" The second image below is a cartoon of a man "violating" a goat with an exaggerated look of pleasure on his face. The caption says, "Nothing good as goatussy, right?"

More things look like they could be horrible, but I don't bother to look at them. I close the page and then my laptop.

The silence around me isn't fair. If the world is going to continue to shit on me every time something nice happens, it could at least not leave me in the quiet with my thoughts screaming terrible things at me.

If life were really fair, I wouldn't have seen that at all, and I wouldn't be sitting here in silence. I would hear masculine laughter and panting breaths, and passionate moans. These cheap, rough sheets should be the softest cotton. My old, flat pillows should be fluffy and full of feathers.

He should be with me, and I should not be alone. I should be a person and not a monster.

I pick up my phone and open the box that says, Liam.

I close my eyes and let the tears build inside them. When I open my eyes, I can see through the blur that he's already texted back.

I breathe in and out several times to try to get my head together. *Am I overreacting?* I already freaked out on him unjustly once at the restaurant, and now again already if I'm in the wrong here. *Damn it.*

> **Me**: Yeah. Come meet me outside my apartment when you get off work. Text me what time.

> **Liam**: Thanks, Jill. I'll see you then. I really miss you.

The table shakes unsteadily as I stand on top of it, thinking things over. Climbing on top of things is one of the few goat features I'll allow only when I am in total distress, like I am now. Letting this little bit of hidden instinct out helps relieve some of the tension inside me. And I'm going to need to be at least a bit more relaxed if I'm going to go out there and not freak out while I admit what a total idiot I've been.

Chapter Twenty-One

Liam

SHE'S SITTING ON THE crumbling concrete stairs of her rundown apartment building. Her knees are pulled up against her chest, arms wrapped around them. In the yellow streetlight, her eyes don't look so odd. Still beautiful as always, though.

"Hey," I say as I walk toward her, hands in the pockets of my wool coat.

"Hey," she replies before patting the spot on the stairs next to her.

I take my seat next to her, unable to resist taking a deep inhale of her sweet and spicy scent as I do. She turns to me and smiles softly, the look on her face tragic enough to break my heart.

"I'm so sorry," she whispers. "I should have known you didn't have anything to do with that. I'm so used to being hurt, I just expect it."

"It's ok." I put my arm around her shoulders, letting her lean into me. "I get it. I'm sorry those people were such shit heads. I should have removed them from that account, but I just didn't even think to check it. It's just not something I look at a lot. I'll be more aware of stuff like that in the future. If you want a future with me, that is."

"I do." She buries her face in my shoulder, angling her head to avoid any unfortunate horn incidents, and takes a deep breath before turning her head back out to face the street. "I really like you, Liam. I know we haven't known each other that long, but I just...*Ugh*, I don't know how to explain it."

I huff out a quiet laugh. "I understand because I feel the same. I think about you all the time. You're just so fucking amazing, Jill. I don't want to be without you."

"Then let's stay together." She wraps her arms around me and holds me tight.

"You have to promise me not to panic and try to leave every time you think there might be a problem, though. I mean, I get why you were upset today, but that's the second time already you tried to leave me, and we've only known each other for a little while. If we're going to be together, you can't break my heart over and over. I've been hurt too, you know? So, just, I don't know, talk to me when you have concerns, and we'll work through stuff. I promise I'll never hurt you on purpose. Okay?" I pull back from her so I can look her in the eyes.

She looks into my eyes for a long moment, seeking something. When it seems she finds it, she nods.

"Okay. I believe you. And I promise we'll communicate when there's a problem instead of me just jumping ship."

I brush her hair back from her face and smile. This beautiful woman has agreed to be mine; she trusts me, and she cares about me. *Fuck,* I think I love her. I lean in and kiss her soft, welcoming lips.

It doesn't take long for our kiss to turn deep, desperate. Our breath grows ragged, our hands searching under our jackets for each other. It's clear we both want *more,* and we want it *now.*

"Jill, I need you now. Let's go to your apartment." My breath comes out in white puffs against her tan neck.

"Not my apartment. I live with my mom and uncle. Sorry," she cringes.

She kisses me again and swings her leg over my lap, lifting her skirt enough to grind her panty-covered pussy against my stiff bulge.

"I want you now," she whines.

"We're out in the open, Jill." I look around us, and my eyes focus on the alley near the next building. "Hold onto me."

I stand, scooping her up with me, and carry her into the alley, far enough away from the street that the light doesn't shine. I look around, listening carefully for any signs of people before setting Jill on her feet.

"Face the wall, baby," I growl into her ear. Getting to be in control with her feels *so good* after my traumatic experience of having no control over my body. That's something to talk about in therapy, though. Right now, all I want to talk about is fucking this gorgeous woman in front of me.

"What?" she squeaks out.

"I said face the wall."

Jill complies, and I follow after, running my hand flat from her neck down to her sweet ass.

"Are you on birth control, sweet girl?" I probably should have asked this before.

"Yes. Are you going to fill me with your cum, Sir? Stuff me with your big, stiff cock, and fuck me until my tight pussy is leaking your seed down my thighs?"

I groan and can't help but grind uselessly against her backside. Who knew she had a mouth like that? I stand back and undo my pants, taking out my achingly hard cock and giving it a few quick strokes.

"That's right, baby girl. I'm going to fill you up. Now let's see that sweet cunt you have waiting for me."

I lift her skirt, revealing the little white, lacy panties she's wearing underneath. The color perfectly sets off the golden color of her skin, and if I wasn't about to sink myself into her perfect flesh, I could stare at it all night. I slide her panties down low enough so that she can spread her legs for me to enter, but not low enough for them to fall to the filthy alley ground. There's not much light in the alley, but what there is reflects off the glistening wetness of her cunt.

"You look ready for me. Are you ready?"

"Yes. Fuck me now, please," she whines.

"You got it."

Chapter Twenty-Two

Jill

LIAM THRUSTS HARD INTO me from behind, grabbing my hips and steadying them so he can use all his force to drive his hard cock into my soft center. I grit my teeth and groan as he pounds into me over and over, our flesh slapping together loudly, the sound obscene in the cool evening air. He hits me over and over again in my most sensitive spots every time he pushes in. My whole body shakes, and I feel like I'm going to fall, my knees growing weak.

Brick scrapes against the zipper of my jacket as my chest is pushed against the wall. Liam holds me firmly against it with one hand, my hip still in the other. I glance over my shoulder and watch his face. It's open in pure ecstasy. His sandy-brown hair falls over his forehead, his mouth open as if in shock. The pink of his cheeks makes him look so young, but the sharp lines of his jaw and the fire in his eyes are all grown man. The beauty of him is too much for me, and for the first time in my life, I come without anyone touching my clit.

"Yes, there you go, that's my girl," Liam grits out. "Squeeze my cock."

"Oh god, keep going. I'm going to milk you of all your cum, don't stop," I plead.

"Fucking hell," he whispers before pounding into me at an increasingly fast pace. He starts to lose his rhythm just slightly before saying, "Touch yourself. Come with me."

"Yes, sir." I obey him, and before long, we're both crying out in bliss.

He shoots load after load of hot, slippery cum into me as my pussy squeezes him. My tail wags uncontrollably, which apparently feels good to Liam because he hisses and shoves himself harder against it.

When we're both done, Liam pulls me to him, letting his softening cock slip out, and his cum drizzle down my thigh before allowing me to slide my panties up. We stand back to front, swaying together as if to music, and I welcome the silence this time.

The silence is only broken by the stammered, hesitant whisper of my name.

"Jill."

"Yeah?"

"I just...I love you. That's all."

"That's all?" I let out a single surprised laugh.

"Yeah. It's whatever," he says with a returned laugh.

"Yeah, well, I love you too." I run the side of my face against his chest, breathing in the scent of him. A smile quirks the edge of my lips. "But it's whatever."

After a bit, there is a crunching sound that spooks both of us. The flash of mirrored eyes reveals nothing more than an old cat, but it scares us out of the alley either way.

"Will you come to my apartment tonight, Jill? I don't want to be apart just yet." He asks me as we stand in front of my building, him leaning down with his forehead against my own and my hands in his.

"Yeah, sure. Just let me get my stuff."

He smiles his bright-white boyish grin and kisses me softly on the lips.

"I'll be right back."

Chapter Twenty-Three

Liam

"ALRIGHT, MS. FLORES, MR. AOKI. Are you ready?"

I hold the needle poised above Ms. Flores's bicep, waiting for both of them to say yes. This separation is a huge deal.

"I'm very ready, Liam," Ms. Flores politely replies.

"Get on with it. I can't wait another second," Mr. Aoki replies through Ms. Flores' voice.

"I understand that feeling," I say with a laugh, though there is still a twinge of pain behind it.

I've been with Jill for four months now, and it's helped to reduce the pain I feel from what happened with Jennifer immensely. But it will never fully go away. That fear of being reduced to nothing, to just an observer in someone else's body, wakes me up at night sometimes still. Thankfully, I've got Jill to hold me until I fall back asleep.

"Here it goes," I say as I plunge the needle into her body and inject the cure I've been working so hard on all these years. Once it's fully injected, I put a bandage on and step back.

A few moments pass where we're all quiet. I've told them what's going to happen, and they know we have to wait. It's tense, and I can feel the anxiety in the air. I know Jill wanted to be here today, but the government still tightly controls anything even remotely related to Heroes and Villains, so I've had her stay far away.

Suddenly, Ms. Flores bends over with a loud grunt. Sweat pours off her face as all her muscles clench.

"There you go. You've got this. Only a moment now," I encourage.

She cries out in pain. This is the toughest part. The physical part doesn't hurt. We don't even really understand the physical aspect, how it works, just that it does. That part is virtually instantaneous. The painful part is separating the two consciousnesses. One lifetime now becoming two again. It feels like a soul being torn apart.

"It hurts," she screams.

"I know," I attempt to soothe her. "It's almost over."

And then it is. Standing next to her on pale, wobbly legs is Mr. Aoki. He starts to fall, but I catch him in time and help him to his seat.

"There you go, Mr. Aoki. Take a minute to sit and get your bearings before trying to do anything much, or you'll fall on your ass," I tell him with a laugh.

"I don't have much of an ass to fall on, so I suppose I should be careful," the thin man replies in a shaky voice.

"Bony ass like his brother had," Ms. Flores replies equally shakily.

All three of us laugh at that. I never met Jill's dad. I know he never got to marry her mom before he passed away, though they were engaged. That he loved her deeply, and everyone knew it. He was waiting until he could give her a big, expensive wedding like he thought she wanted. She says she would have married him in the courthouse and been just fine.

I swear I'll never let money get in the way of making Jill happy. So, I used mine to get her what would do that, and I did it right away.

Chapter Twenty-Four

Jill

THE WINTER SUN SHINES down on the snow-covered fields, turning everything blindingly white. I shield my eyes and turn away, watching my new sheepdog play in the fluffy white stuff at my feet.

"Oh, Jim, you silly boy, you're gonna get all wet," I say as I scratch his head. I know it's a weird name for a sheepdog, but that was his name at the animal rescue, and he responds to it, so it stayed.

Jim licks my hand and bounds away, rolling around in the snow and making happy yelps. I shake my head and laugh at the silly thing. I won't be laughing when I have to deal with the sopping wet mess later, but for now, it's cute.

I close my eyes and listen to the sounds around me. I hear the soft sounds of chickens clucking in their coop. Cows are mooing in the barn. The bell on the neck of my troublemaking sheep is ringing. I've only had this farm for a few weeks, and already, these sounds are my norm. They comfort me. They're the sounds of home. And it's all thanks to Liam.

Speaking of Liam, I hear a car coming down the highway, then down the long gravel road leading to our house. *Our* house. It didn't take long for us to decide to move in together. Everyone said we were crazy, but we don't care. We've both been through some *really* crazy shit. This is not that. This is love.

The car door closes. Two doors. Three. I open my eyes, my mouth splitting my face in the biggest grin.

"Mom? Uncle Sal?" I ask as I turn around.

And yes, they're both there. Whole and individual people. Tears begin to stream from my eyes as I run through the grass and gravel to get to my mom first. Sal meets us in our embrace, and all three of us cry together. We hold each other and cry for several minutes, a necessary release of emotion built up over years of holding it in, trying to be strong for each other. But finally, we quiet our sobs and step back from one another, just a little.

"I'm so happy," I say, my voice still shaking from crying. My mom just nods and wipes her nose on a tissue she pulled from who knows where.

"I'm so happy I could dance if I trust remembering how to operate this body well enough. It feels so odd now. Who knew I was so tall?" He looks down at his feet and shakes his head.

I can't help but laugh. He is nearly a foot taller than my mom, so I can imagine that getting used to moving as a tall, skinny man, rather than a short, curvy woman, after four years might take a bit.

"I'm telling you, these arms and legs are like noodles. First thing I'm doing is thickening up." He pats his belly, and my mom joins me in the laughter.

"Well, Jill is an excellent cook. Maybe she'll make something special as a welcome back treat tonight to help you along," Liam suggests.

I hold out my arms to welcome Liam into my embrace. We hold one another for a moment before separating, and I place my hand on his cheek.

"You bet I will. Anything you all want."

"Speaking of wants," Liam says, face turning sheepish. "My dad wants to meet your mom."

My mom's brown face turns ghostly white. She puts a petite hand on Uncle Sal's arm to steady herself.

"Do you mean...you mean...Honor Man wants to meet *me*?" she asks.

Liam rolls his eyes and huffs. "Yes. His real name is Ronald. He's not that exciting."

"Not that exciting. Please," she replies as if personally offended. She then pauses, places her hands on her heart, and looks as if stars are in her eyes. "*Ronald*. What a beautiful name."

"Oh no," I grumble. "I'll never hear the end of this, will I?"

Liam chuckles. "Nope. Sorry."

"You're lucky I love you." I pinch his ass, making him blush as he looks around to make sure no one saw.

"I am lucky. I love you, Jill."

We head into our house on our farm, where flowers don't get us in trouble, smiles don't falter, and our love can be whatever, forever.

Bonus

A Sneak Peek Six Years into the Future of the Mashieverse.

Notorious Villain Tabitha Lima, Also Known as Poison Princess, Sits Down for an Interview with Jenna O'Leary of the Capital City Tribune.

Tabitha

"It was short for 'Darkest Kiss.' He thought the meaning was obvious between the name and his ability. He claimed his power was *the most intimate, most private act possible—no kiss more hidden in any shadow'* or some dumb thing like that."

The image of Darkiss striding back and forth across the living room, passionately rambling on about his name, enters my mind. The other girls in the house made faces at me from across the room, trying to get me to laugh, so I'd get into trouble with him.

The corner of my mouth twitches upward at the memory. I should call the girls, see how they're doing. First, I have to get this interview over with. I clear my throat, then finish answering the question.

"But of course, people didn't understand his name. How would they? That *really* annoyed him. It made me laugh, honestly."

"And why did you find that funny, Tabitha?" the reporter asks.

She bites down on the tip of her glasses. I think she's trying to look smart, holding them delicately in her hand like that. No one holds them that way naturally. It's worse, actually: I don't even think those are prescription lenses. The old me would call her out on it. Mock her. This new, reformed me graciously ignores it and answers her question.

"He insisted we all have *obvious* Villain names. Ones everyone would understand—Klaire Voyant, Angelust, Stonecrash, et cetera. After all, you need brand recognition if you want to be remembered. So, when no one could figure out what Darkiss meant, it was just so ironic." I can't help but crack a smile.

"Wait, so you're saying Darkiss forced you to take on the moniker Poison Princess?"

The smile immediately drops from my face. How I despise that name.

"Yeah. Good old *Darren* sure did. He threatened to mash us if we didn't use them."

"Then, assuming his threats were serious—"

"They were *always* serious." I might say disrespectful things about Darkiss sometimes, but I would never say he was a liar. I don't particularly like it when anyone else does, either.

The reporter's face pales as she looks at mine, seeing the warning. Her eyelids flutter as she wets her lips to carry on.

"So, Ms. Lima, he could have included you and the other three in The Big Mash-Up—yet he chose not to. How does that make you feel?"

"I'm not fond of him, if that's what you're asking. We weren't friends. The only reason he didn't transform us like he did everyone else in the city was that he needed his little army."

Darkiss always needed his sycophants. After he unleashed his power on the world and became enemy number one, he needed us more than ever.

"I see. Can you tell us why you were chosen to be one of his comrades?"

Not like he had much of a choice. Does she think powered people grow on trees? He found the desperate, pissed off ones—end of story.

She leans forward, the faux pearl necklace swaying across her blouse. Wait. No, those are real pearls. Fake glasses, real pearls. Got it.

"I can't legally discuss that as part of the Villain rehabilitation program." It's my go-to for every question I don't want to answer, but this time it's true.

After picking a piece of lint from my black— *always black*—pants, I cross my arms and lean back in my chair. I admittedly get self-conscious every time I have to mention being in the program. It's embarrassing.

When I was an active Villain, people feared and respected me. That I can handle. Enjoy, on occasion. Being a *former* Villain is something entirely different.

"Understood. I also understand that you can't tell us any specific details about why you chose to use your powers to be a Villain, rather than a Hero," she says, pausing for a moment on the off chance I might answer.

Nope. Can't, and even if I could, it's a stupid question. How would I be a superhero with poison skin as my power?

"Is there anything you're allowed to tell us about why you chose to commit the acts you did in the days *after* The Big Mash-Up? The optometrist, for example?"

She holds a pen to paper and waits. She hasn't taken notes this entire time, and I know she won't begin to. This is all on camera—her notepad is just for show.

"Why did I do it all? Well, you're right—I'm not allowed to talk publicly about the details."

Because, Ms. Reporter, the answer isn't very pleasant.

The government only wants people to know the good things they do—like turning *hardened criminals* like me into productive citizens. None of the unpleasant things. I've been warned, in no uncertain terms, to keep my mouth shut. I'm certainly not allowed to tell reporters how they took me out of a foster home, tortured me, and spliced me with dart frog DNA. If I want a life outside of prison, that is—or a life at all. So, I tell her what I *am* allowed to say.

"I had a very, very difficult upbringing. I'll leave it at that."

The reporter smiles, a lot of unnaturally white teeth contrasting sharply with her cakey, orange-toned makeup.

"Thank you for your time, Poi—Tabitha. I wish you the best of luck as a free citizen of our great city."

I don't miss the fact that the reporter swallows hard, smile faltering briefly, before she reaches out to shake my velvet-gloved hand. If I were her, I'd be nervous too. One brush of my skin could cause her severe pain and hallucination. Touch me longer than that, and she'd die. But, luckily for her, I am wearing gloves. Two pairs—just in case.

I grip her hand, smile, and shake.

"Thank you, Ms. O'Leary. It was a pleasure meeting you."

Thank You

Thank you so much to my beta readers, my ARC readers, my PAs, my friends, and everyone who helped me get this book out both the first time and the second time. You're all awesome. Special shout outs to: Latrexa, Cassie, Shannon, Vera, Michaela, May, Alijay, Tee, Ellie, and Ginger.

Want More Mashieverse?

FIND OUT WHAT HAPPENS in Capital City six years after Goat Girl in the next Mashieverse book, Poison Princess.

He's the only one immune to her deadly touch.

A decade after The Big Mash-Up, Capital City is safer than ever. The Villain rehabilitation program is a success!

...So they say.

Recently released from Gnistra Lake State Penitentiary, Tabitha Lima—AKA Poison Princess—knows intimately the many flaws Capital City tries to hide. Their government made her who she is, after all.

Gave her poison skin. Made her untouchable. Turned her into a monster.

An opossum Mashie with a Heroes and Villains kink, Henry can't believe his luck when he meets *the* Poison Princess—no, *Tabitha*. She's the tall, curvy, powerful woman of his dreams.

When they find out he's the only person immune to her poison touch, he's determined to find the key to her heart.

But her trust is locked up tight, even if she's not currently behind bars.

www.ingramcontent.com/pod-product-compliance
Lightning Source LLC
Chambersburg PA
CBHW060337310726
48976CB00007B/2586